Acknowledgement

Thank you, Roger T. Quinn Jr., friend and fellow Beach Author Network author for originally sharing the premise for this story with me several years ago and giving me permission to use it.

T. Allen Winn's

Guns and Ashes

Four Friends at a Fish Fry

A Hardy Look

Hardy Bovine did things his way, in his timeframe. It mattered not to him whether you liked it, agreed with it or chastised him for doing it. Many called him just plain ornery, but a friend was a friend. Such a friend was Steele who stuck by him loyally through thick and thin. Those who chastised Hardy only did it one time. Hardy had a not so tactful way of telling you it wasn't really any of your business what he did, what he thought or how he acted. In his words, 'He didn't need any man or woman telling him what'fer when it came right down to his business or his opinions.' He spoke his mind; called them like he saw them and if he didn't like something nobody was going to convince him otherwise. Call him colorful, an obscene foul mouth old coot or even worse if you felt real *froggy* and ready to get your butt kicked. Yeah, that's right. Hardy Bovine never shied away from a good fight, verbal ones and just plain scuffling in the dirt. Never pick a fight with a pig in the mud. You'll come up on the short end so says Hardy. Steele Dillon, a complete opposite by nature had to be pushed hard to retaliate. An recent incident with his truck had pushed him well beyond his tolerance level.

Rite of passage, Hardy would spout it to anyone that wanted to listen. He would speak his mind whether you wanted to hear him out or not. This here day, second Tuesday of August, he was two months and three days from seeing his eightieth year of being above dirt. He was still as healthy as a plow mule and almost as stubborn. He had plenty of smarts between his ears. Hardy hadn't got him none of that Old Timer's sickness like some of his old buddies, not that he could recall anyway. He still dipped snuff, drank his fair share of George Dickel Whisky, green label, 90 proof, preferred, and hankered now and then for a little poke over at Miss Lottie's. She operated a business that catered to a man's needs, especially one with plenty of green in his billfold. Paying for it suited Hardy just fine. There was no courtship and no ties once it was done. He sure didn't need no live-in cook and maid making his life miserable. He could take care of that just fine and still hunt, fish, drink and gamble without a gospel spewing woman putting up a fuss and raising a ruckus. Steele didn't walk his pal's path and let slide whatever Hardy felt like

5

doing. Steele figured that someone his age had earned the rite to just be himself. Hardy shied away from church and the bible, but he did not hold it against Steele for seeking the spiritual calling.

Hardy drew the line at having children. Married or not, which he wasn't and never had been, he had no hankering to be a daddy. Snot nose young'uns had no more business in his life than he had in theirs. He was the furthest thing from a role model. Don't be fooled though. He could have taught the little brats a thing or two had he been so unlucky to have one. Unruly chaps had no place in his life, and he wasn't shy about telling a parent what'fer if they let them run wild like a bunch of crazed banshees. There was nothing worse than him trying to enjoy a peaceful meal at the Tasty Platter Diner when Ronnie-Lee brought her litter of screaming and unruly brood in. It got old, her slapping at them and yelling meaningless threats all the while they were bouncing off the walls. It only took Hardy grabbing the first one by the arm, giving him or her a little friendly yank and a look, and then telling them to sit down and shut the hell up until he finished his meal, to be an attention getter for the rest of the little buggers. Ronnie-Lee didn't question his technique or overreach in doing so. She might have even been a little appreciative if truth be known. She didn't have a man in her life. Any feller probably hightailed it given the circumstances of her unfortunate way. He surely wasn't about to volunteer for daddy duty, even though she was still a looker after popping out six.

Steele had never been married either, but he was a bit more tolerable of unruly children than his old friend. Marriage was not off limits. Pretty simple, he had never met a woman that had smitten his fancy. He was only thirty-eight, plenty of time to get hitched if ever the right one did come along. Steele wasn't looking so one would have to stumble across his path for him to take notice. Some thought the age difference between him, and Hardy made for an unlikely friendship. Neither Steele nor Hardy gave it much thought. They got along just fine and how others saw it did not hold water.

Yes sir'ree Bob, Hardy Bovine was his own man. He wasn't handsome, but who was at his age? His face left no doubt to those who looked upon it that he had been rode hard and put up wet. He had earned ever wrinkle and every scar fair and square. He had the stories to back it up. After putting away a pint of George green label his tongue loosened up a tad and he would lay claim to all his conquests, his brawls and back breaking labor that landed him to where he stood today. Hardy wasn't a believer in taking handouts. He always gave an honest day's work for what was owed him. It just right down ticked him off to see folks taking advantage of a free ride, thinking that they were entitled to food stamps and unemployment checks, acting all pitiful and poor and broken down. 'Get off your lazy ass and find a job' he would fuss. Jobs are out there for the taking if you're not sorry and worthless like a pile of green blowfly infested horse manure. Steele shared the same sentiment. Work ethics were not something to be taken lightly.

Hardy was a man's man, stout with no sagging chicken wings under his arms. He got around without the help of a cane or walker, unlike most his age. He spat in father times face, refusing to be just the next old fart shuffling along, biding his time until the Grim Reaper laid claim to his rickety old bones. There was no real method to the magic of him staying healthy. He didn't exercise or eat right. It must just be in his genes or something. He rarely ever got sick and seldom had any nagging aches and pains. Hardy was thankful for still having his health and he didn't give thanks nearly enough, not a churchgoer by nature. Contrary to his actions and how he pushed back when Steele brought up the subject, he did believe in the good book and did mostly what it said you were supposed to do. Well, most, including Steele, might not see it the way he did but for sure he hadn't killed or coveted or stolen. Most of the important stuff was abided by in his mind. What he did down at Miss Lottie's didn't count. He looked on it as giving back and supporting hard working women folks, earning their keep the best they could. Who was he to argue with how they made their living? Steele shied away from that path, giving Miss Lottie wide berth. He agreed with Hardy. Her business was her business, and she would have to reckon with it when the time came.

August days, dog days what some called them, could get pert near unbearable in the low country of South Carolina. Didn't make no mind to ole Hardy though, living in Ridgeville, about 35 miles northwest of Charleston and a stone's throw from Monks Corner where he had been born into to this world. Ridgeville was known for the Lieber Correctional Institution, the states depository for those sentenced to death. Hardy had a fondness for the penitentiary, having worked as a guard in Columbia's Broad River Correctional Institution and now at Lieber. It was unusual for a man his age to be working at a prison. Hardy wasn't your run of the mill eighty-year-old. Might be that the warden thought he was somewhat of a novelty having him there. There had been several news segments shot about him and he had appeared in a few magazine articles. Fact was, so far, he had not been a liability and could actually hold his own against guards fifty some odd years his junior. Steele worried about him working at the prison but never brought it up.

Steele was a history buff and had researched the prison. Lieber was the state's institute for housing men on death's row. From 1912 to January 1990 male death row inmates were housed in the Central Correctional Institution (CCI). BRCI held male death row inmates from January 1990 to April 12, 1997, when male death row inmates were moved to Lieber. From 1912 to 1986 executions were carried out at CCI. On April 12, 1997, Death Row inmates were moved to Lieber Correctional Institution. This move provided better management controls and ensured that the correctional staff who deal with those inmates on a daily basis were not the same individuals charged with the responsibility of carrying out the death warrant as ordered by the state.

Steele was also fascinated by the execution process. By State statute, witnesses are designated for executions according to the following guidelines: There are three media witnesses, one print, one broadcast, and one representative from the dominant wire service (Associated Press in this area). The family of the victim is allowed three witnesses. If there are more than one victim, the Corrections' Director may reduce the number of family representatives to one representative for each victim's family. Further, if there are more than two victims, the Director may restrict the total number of victims' representatives present in accordance with the space limitation of the Capital Punishment Facility. The law also allows for a minister of the gospel, the counsel for the inmate, the chief law enforcement officer (or designee) and the solicitor or assistant solicitor for the county where the offense occurred to be present.

The process of ending the lives of those sentenced to death disturbed Steele. He and Hardy had many lengthy discussions on the fact, justified or not. Legislation signed into law on June 8, 1995, provided the option of lethal injection as a means of executing a condemned person. Hardy explained how the chemicals necessary to carry out lethal injection were handled, stored and disposed of in accordance with a strict protocol that limits the number of individuals who have access to the chemicals. Hardy was a man that believed a man should die by the manner in which he murdered. He figured this way the victim received proper justification, the one what killed them being killed the same way. He leaned toward frying them in the electric chair rather than allowing them to ease out of the world by injection. Injection was too humane for his liking for those worthless varmints that had taken lives without remorse. Steele stayed clear of these discussions because they only seemed to rile the old man. Hang'um high he would often say.

Hardy took pride in his prison job while there, his face being about the last one those being put to death laid eyes on before the electrical juice fried their worthless good for nothing, Godforsaken souls. Hardy didn't have much tolerance when it came to lawbreakers, especially those murderous scoundrels responsible for innocent law-abiding peoples' deaths. Cop killers just made him want to be the one what volunteered to pull the power lever. He likened his role to that of the guards in that *Green Mile* movie. *Tom Hanks*, now that was a fine actor in his book. Hardy liked watching those *Bosom Buddy* reruns. As cantankerous as Hardy Bovine might be, he wasn't a law breaker by nature. Sure, he colored outside the lines when it came to gambling, womanizing and drinking but by his view, none of these vices hurt anybody and surely didn't get nary a person killed or raped or robbed. Fighting and tussling came naturally but he drew the line when it came to maiming or murdering. Steele, not a fighter, preferred talking his way out of volatile situations. Well, that ended with his truck been trashed at the shop.

In two months and three days he would celebrate another birthday. Some might consider it milestone but to Hardy it would just be another day like any other day in his life. He might smoke him a cigar and sip some George Dickel but otherwise it would just come and go with no fanfare, no cake, and no damn candles to huff and puff until extinguished. A cake, if he actually had one, would be declared a fire hazard if loaded up with his lifetime worth of little wax candles. He wasn't that much into sweets anyway other than having him a big ole bowl of Widow Jenkins's homemade *nanner puddin* every now and then. Just thinking about hers made his mouth moisten up and if he didn't get his mind off it, he would be slobbering like a red fox with rabies. He sure didn't want to get caught looking like Gabriel Turner, his ole hunting buddy, what had landed in the old folks' home, bedridden wearing those depends and drooling like a three-month-old chap, bless his heart. Widow woman Jenkins had taken a fancy to him, always wooing him and wanting him to show her favors. He'd save his favors for down at Miss Lottie's where the women folk were young and rounded in all the right places, not shaped like the Liberty Bell, eighty-three-year-old Widow Jenkins. Steele knew how Hardy felt about birthdays and made light of it for the most part by just wishing him a happy one. He would oblige him by smoking a cigar and sharing one drink.

The position of the shadows on his front porch told Hardy it must be nearly four o'clock, the summer daylight more than half gone. It was still hot as blue blazes but a man ain't healthy if he ain't bleeding ignorant oil. That's what Hardy called senseless sweating, bleeding ignorant oil. His daddy, Big John Bovine, rest his sorry soul, had always called it that, saying '*Boy, if you got no better sense than to stay out there under that blazing hot sun and bleed ignorant oil, then you best not bring your stinky self to my supper table without running a rag through it.*' Ole Hardy broke out into a grin recalling those long-gone times with Daddy John. Today just seemed to be one of those days where his mind just wandered about aimlessly from one subject to another. Sometimes he just couldn't help it. Might be that the Old Timer's disease sneaking up on him, him forgetting what happened an hour ago but remembering stuff that had long been buried in his head. It didn't much matter one way or the other. It was his mind to do what he wanted with it. He didn't have to answer to nobody but Hardy Bovine and the maker above. Steele was always amazed by the man's sharp mind and equally stout body. He seemed ageless.

Right now, Hardy had to decide the important stuff like figuring on what he was having for supper. What were his choices? What did he have a hankering for? Lunch had been a fried baloney meat and mater toasted sandwich. His daddy garnished it with a slice of onion, pickle and lettuce. His bread had been smeared thick with Dukes mayonnaise. His side was a bag of hot pig skins. He had chased that down with a quart Mason jar of ice-cold sweet tea. Cornbread and buttermilk sounded good for supper, but he was too hungry to take the time to prepare a cast iron skillet of cornbread right now. Well, he could take a short cut and use Frito's corn chips instead in his bowl of buttermilk but even that wasn't quite hitting the spot. A sloppy cheeseburger and fries sounded good, but he wasn't up to getting out and driving over to The Burger Barn. Hardy stood first in front of the open refrigerator door and then the pantry door, waiting for something to snag his interest. Nothing did. Frustrated and just a tad agitated, he plucked a can of mustard laced sardines and a box of saltines from the pantry. The combo would hold him a while. Steele was always amazed by Hardy's constitution. He could eat and digest almost anything.

Meal prepared, he settled into his old recliner with a can of Blue Ribbon. He then clicked the remote and surfed until he found the *Andy Griffith Show*, airing one of his favorites with *Ernest T. Bass* pining for *Charlene Darling* and *Briscoe Darling and the Darling Brothers* preferring *Andy* instead. He knew everything that was going to happen and could have probably quoted every single line if he had wanted to, but he still laughed his ass off as if seeing it for the very first time. Simple stuff always struck his funny bone. He still liked *Gomer* better than *Goober Pyle* and *Ellen Walker* the pharmacist, *Andy's* first gal friend, better than *Helen Crump*, the schoolteacher. Hardy had a fondness for Daphne *and Skippy*, the fun girls from several episodes. *Daphne* reminded him just a tad of Miss Lottie. *Otis Campbell* was a hoot too, taking the liberty to lock his drunken ass up in that jail cell instead of going home. Funny though, *Otis* was about the only married feller on the show, and it was

11

supposed to be one of the best family shows on at the time. Steele, when visiting, would sit and watch old episodes with Hardy and laugh just as hard over the gags they both knew were coming.

Hardy caught himself thinking back on the conversation he had struck up with one of the prisoners, an old fool, Elrod Long, caught one time too many selling bootleg and cigarettes to minors. Elrod had been busted red handed stealing the liquor and cigarettes from Joe McClellan's Grocery and then selling them to those teenagers willing to pay top dollar. Hardy didn't take a liking to many prisoners, but he made an exception of ole Elrod, pretty harmless compared to most of the sorry ones incarcerated under his watch. Elrod was four years older than him. Swapping stories, having a smoke and a friendly checker game had been a daily ritual for them. Checkers had all but become a lost art, everyone caught up in those fancy video games. Hardy had grown up on board games and playing cards, rolling a few dice. The old ways were still the best ways in his book. Elrod appreciated the same sort of stuff too. The old coot had tried once and only once, attempting to bribe him into smuggling some whisky, but Hardy had quickly drawn the line making saying it wasn't going to happen, not on his watch or by him. Elrod never posed the question again.

It was today's topic during their daily checker game that he couldn't seem to shake. It was just one of those things that dog you and won't let you be. Hardy wasn't one who liked to dwell on important stuff. Life was just too short to get hung up on serious pondering, especially topics concerning dying. The way he looked at it, dying was just a part of living. You did both. One was the beginning and the other was the ending. Everyone does it sooner or later. He preferred later, postponing it for as long as possible, but still knowing when your time came it would happen without you having much say so about it. It really was not any more complicated than that, end of story. That's why he didn't think on it, worry or fret about it and just took every blessed day as it came. Well, he had done it that way until Elrod Long had messed him up royally. Blue Ribbon wasn't cutting it. He fetched a fresh bottle of George Dickel, something he didn't normally do while on his prison work schedule.

Right now, wasn't a normal occasion and he justified his actions thusly. He cursed Elrod Long for placing him in this predicament.

Hardy bottomed out his glass in one swig and quickly poured a second, no ice, no dice, he would often say. Five in the morning would roll around early but that didn't really concern him. He had never been late nor had he missed a single day of work in his life. It just wasn't in his make-up to take his responsibilities lightly, even for a feller who didn't take life seriously. Some said he had screwed up priorities. What some said was their opinion and he certainly wasn't going to change his ways over opinions. Like him or not, that was your choice. He lived his life not based on popularity contests or pleasing those around him. Don't get him wrong, he took pride in his prison position, but he wasn't an ass kisser. He abided by what rules he was supposed to do and wasn't a slacker. He hated slackers and wasn't shy about calling them out if they didn't pull their fair share of the load. Most folks either respected him or feared him. Either of them worked for Hardy. What he liked about his best friend Steele was that he was not a slacker either. Steele, to his reckoning, was as loyal to his job as the day was long.

He turned the bottle on the table, staring at it like one of those gypsy crystal balls, looking for answers possibly or just thinking on what Elrod Long had said. Most conversations didn't bother him. After all they were just conversations and once the last word was spoken then so ended the talk. This one continued to dog him though and he didn't like being hounded like a rabbit running from a pack of beagles. There was no hole to hide in and besides, Hardy wasn't the hiding type. He took things on full throttle, head on and bullied his way through. This was his problem-solving technique. Just deal with it and get it behind you as fast as possible. Life was too short to dither. Life is too short, fitting mantra considering that conversation with Elrod Long. Like it or not, face it or refuse to face it, Hardy was well down the backside of life's slope. He still felt good and fit but reaching a hundred was most likely a pipedream. Not many people made it to that ripe old age and those what did had to depend on somebody taking care of them. Hardy didn't want or need anybody making a fuss over him. If it got to where he couldn't take care of his needs, he'd just as soon check out, cash in and call it quits. He wasn't quite sure how he would handle that situation gracefully if it ever came. He and Steele had conversed often over this quandary. There was no clear solution. Fact was, face it if it arrived.

He did believe a person had the right to pick if your life went to hell in a hand basket. He wasn't exactly a bible totter, but he knew it wasn't right to take your own life either. Right is right. Wrong is wrong. It's just that simple. The good book said you don't pick your time to go and just do it yourself. Still, Hardy didn't like the prospects of some day becoming a drooling vegetable with others feeding him and changing his diapers. He had seen another buddy Benny Phelps, venture down that road and vowed that it would never ever happen to him. Benny had landed in one of those nursing homes. The premise scared the hell out of him. He had no close family and couldn't fathom strangers handling his personal needs like some helpless little newborn. He poured another shot and downed it, but the image didn't go away in a mere swallow of gut-wrenching whisky. How had he allowed his mind to get caught up in the spider web? He knew exactly how. It was Elrod's fault for bringing it up.

Out of nowhere, he had a bad hankering for a bowl of Widow Jenkins' *nanner puddin*. It might help his old thinker or might not, but it would satisfy a sudden sweet tooth. Hardy settled for a banana flavored Moon Pie instead. It was not quite the same by a long shot. The problem at hand, what was he going to do about that seed Elrod Long had furrowed deeply in his head. It surely didn't look as if it was just going to go away. Out of sight out of mind just wasn't cutting it. He didn't have anyone to talk it through with, not that this was something he would have wanted to discuss with someone else besides maybe Steele. Most of his friends were either dead, not long for it or just not capable of carrying on a decent conversation because either they no longer knew who he was or who they were. Steele remained his true confidant. He considered phoning him, but this wasn't something he wanted to converse about on the phone. He could ask Steele to drop by but it being a work night didn't seem a fair time to share his troubles with his friend. Nope, he would have to deal with this in his lonesome, thanks to Elrod Long.

Hardy had always thought cancer eating you away was the worst kind of sickness, but that was before he had gotten real up close and personal with that mind stealing disease. A man could be healthy as a mule but if your mind didn't know any better then what good did it really get you. Poor old Benny Phelps was the perfect example, a big ole turnip just plopped down in that hospital bed, dependent on others to tell him what to do or do it for him. It was a mighty shame but what could you do? Doctors said there was no cure. Alzheimer's was something that had to run its course. They shoot horses, if putting them out to pasture ain't doable, don't they? Dying or a person's brain turning to mush was the least of it, so had pointed out Elrod Long. There was other stuff to consider, and Hardy hadn't really taken the time to think on it, figuring he had no next of kin to be worried with it. Dead is dead. Gone is gone. He just figured it wouldn't matter to him what happened afterwards, just somebody else's problem. That wasn't the way Elrod Long saw it and he was a man passionate about his convictions. Hardy was taught to always respect his elders even if they weren't that much older than him.

Hardy glanced over at the wall clock; almost 10:30. It was pert near time for him to be thinking about retiring for the night with a long twelve-hour shift ahead of him tomorrow staring him in the face. The old brain just wasn't cooperating with what his body needed though, compliments of Elrod Long. Getting one's affairs in line didn't seem like something he should be doing tonight but dwelling he was. He wasn't sick. He wasn't even feeling bad. If truth be told, George Dickel had him feeling very little right now. He might be feeling it in the morning if he didn't wean off that bottle before it was too late. What to do, what to do and why did it have to be decided tonight anyway? What if he up and went to bed and never woke up, that's why. Stranger things have happened; a person feeling perfectly fine one minute and deader than hell the next. Sometimes there were no warning signs, no nothing, just over and out. That's why people had wills to cover this sort of thing when the unexpected happened. He and Steele had one more thing in common; no family around to tend to what might need tending if it happened. Steele did not have a will either. Two wrongs did not make a right.

Hardy, like Steele, hadn't been much on having a will for one reason and one reason alone. Who were they going to leave their stuff to anyway? Hardy didn't have any next of kin. Hardy's thinking, once I'm gone it don't much matter what happens to my stuff. I can't take it with me. Let somebody figure it out and fight over it; not much really to fight over either. Why not just tell Steele everything he owned belonged to him when he passed? No, it was not his way to figure on dying and all. A will wasn't what really had his brain all tied in knots, but it was kind of connected to what Elrod Long had insinuated over checkers. Last will and testament are what he had referred to during their conversation. Elrod had a will and had his affairs all planned out. He had settled it while incarcerated. He probably had the extra time to think about it and act on it while locked up behind bars.

Pure rubbish, he didn't need go down this path. He didn't even like thinking about it and it wasn't because it made him squeamish, because it didn't. Nothing did. Hardy wasn't afraid of anything and had none of those phobias a lot of folks get their panties all in a wad about. It was all pure silliness as far as he was concerned. Still, why had this gotten so deeply embedded under his doggone skin? Maybe that had been Elrod Long's intent, to rattle his cage for a good laugh. He was probably elbowing other inmates, bragging about it. Well Hardy wasn't about to be anybody's cheap entertainment, especially not for a bunch of jailbirds. Elrod might have just crossed the line. He would have to find somebody else to play checkers with if this was his idea of a joke. He hadn't looked like he was yanking his chain though. The old boy appeared dead serious about the conversation. Maybe he should just give him the benefit of the doubt and let it be. Besides, admitting it had bothered him might just be what he was waiting for if it had been intended otherwise. Steele weighing in might sway his thinking. He stared at the phone but thought otherwise.

So, what now? Should he think more on it or try to catch some shuteye? Like he really had a choice, his old brain wasn't going to let go until he came to some understanding with it. That was a fact, no denying it. The seed had been planted, end of that story, thanks to Elrod Long. Hardy thought better when he put it down on paper, so he found his note pad and a pencil. He never used a pen when he was doing his thinking. A pen made things permanent. An eraser offered the option of a do over, a way to fix it if it wasn't going the way he saw it. He had to use a computer at work, but he did just what he had to do and no more. He wasn't much on new fangled toys anyway. The warden made them all carry cell phones. His was for receiving calls. He never used it for outgoing ones. He still had his land line and hardly ever used it either other than calling Steele or ordering a pizza. The only reason he had basic cable, his antenna atop his house no longer provided a good picture. He still had a clunky old box style television, long after everyone else had gone to those flat faced ones. Nope, technology didn't much interest Hardy Bovine. Procrastination, he was stalling, thinking about everything but what would put an end to his pondering. He was good at that, unless it was work related, which this really wasn't.

The pencil hovered over the note pad, the point not yet making contact. Touching the tip on the pad would instigate him writing something. Was he really ready for this? Hardy had this thing about that. If he once started writing he couldn't stop until he finished what he started. Committing to it made it real and obsession kicked in then, finish it and fix it, or at least make a list to choose from later. It had to be done that way or else, he couldn't just walk away from it. To him it was worse than not finishing a conversation, his way of working it out, getting it from inside his head and where he could see it more clearly. Maybe it came from him being a loner. Well, it didn't really matter where it came from. It was his way and there was no getting around it once he had his mind made up to go this route. He touched the tip of the pencil on the paper, done, here we go, hell or high water, Katie bar the doors, ready or not here comes old Hardy full throttle, peddle to the metal, no turning back.

He first scribbled, *how to die*, but then erased that, not happy with his chosen words. Everybody dies sooner or later. That's not what this is about, not according to Elrod Long. This was definitely not going to be his last will and testament. That sounded too much like he was preparing to die, which he wasn't. He wasn't even close unless the Man up above was keeping secrets from him. Nothing he could do about it if He was. He thought on it some more. What

17

happens when you go belly up? That all depends on a couple of options, a peaceful departure or one caused by a horrendous accident. Dying by fire or a real bad car wreck for instance could leave not much to look at; thusly the undertaker usually suggested a closed coffin in those cases. Reckon this really had not that much to do with how a person bought the big one. Dead was dead anyway you paint it. No denying now, he should have called Steele to weigh in on it.

Hardy touched the pencil point on the paper again, this time scribbling burial preferences. Were they really preferences? He hadn't given the *how to* much thought until that stupid conversation over checkers with Elrod Long. It had been the usual friendly game and hardly ever did they talk about important stuff, not even politics, religion or real personal stuff. Well not until today, but wasn't this burial crap both personal and sort of religious by nature? Elrod Long, right out of the blue and with no warning, had point blank asked him how he had planned to be put to rest. He pointed how that both of them were long of tooth and couldn't have that many more years under their belts. This had been a far cry from the run of the mill checker talk. Hardy always figured that was a no-brainer and someone else's problem, not his. Elrod had decided his fate, cremation, no fuss, no coffin and less expensive, not that he had to worry about paying for it when he was gone. He had even picked out a fancy urn to display his remains, had a photograph of it and a few words he wanted inscribed on it. He wanted his only child, a daughter to perch it atop his old barn, affix it right next to the eagle weathervane. What he wanted and what his daughter did after he was gone would be anybody's guess, so said Elrod Long. She would have to live with the consequences if she didn't abide by his wishes.

Hardy wrote down the word *cremation* just because it was on his mind at the time, not because he was considering it or had ever considered it. What did that really leave as a choice other than a regular burial in a coffin? With a coffin though you had to pick out one or most did ahead of time or their kinfolk did after they died. He certainly hadn't drafted a choice and had no kin to pick for him after he was gone. He dreaded the premise of milling around in a funeral home and shopping for one that best fit. Even with cremation you had to select one of those fancy jars for storage and then decide who would be so lucky to get it and where to put it. He should have just left this alone and let somebody else burden themselves with the decision. Too late though, he had commenced writing it down and now he had to finish what he had started. Embalming preserved you as is but too many *as is* people didn't look so good. Few looked like themselves and folks just loved peeking inside those caskets to see how you measured up. One thing for sure, he didn't want an open coffin and a bunch of freeloading gawkers deciding how good or bad he rested inside.

So, what about cremation then? Some shied away from this saying what if you really needed your body to cross over into the hereafter. How could you be certain one way or the other? Those who died couldn't exactly tell you what had happened; that is unless you believe in ghosts and those mediums who say they can talk to the dead. Hardy didn't buy any of the mumbo jumbo junk. Dead was dead, body and bones to dust eventually. Placing the pencil behind his left ear, he poured another shot of whisky just to clear his head. He placed the empty glass down. He thumped his fingers on the table, searching for a solution to his problem, the one instilled by Elrod Long, his ex-checker playing buddy, if he so decided to quit playing but that wasn't his concern right now. He underlined the word cremation twice and then circled it for good measure. Hardy rubbed his chin. Sometimes that helped his thinking process, that and another shot of whisky. He reminded himself that this was way too much whisky consumption for a work night.

He sucked in a deep breath and wrote down what he reckoned could be his final answer. It had come to him right out of the blue but the more he thought on it the more it made perfectly good sense. He liked it so much he decided right then and there that he wanted it notarized as his last wishes. Mabel Harrison, the receptionist at Lieber, was a notary public, so tomorrow he would make this official and place it in his bank security drawer for safe keeping. He jotted down just under his decision that he better tell somebody about the bank drawer and where to find the key just in case he bought the farm without warning. That person would be Steele. What were friends for, and Steele was the only one he entrusted with this. He

19

could now settle in for what was left of a night's sleep. The whisky would help him drift off but come morning it would be another story. Still, confident about his decision, he would rest peacefully until the alarm invaded his privacy.

Lunch time arrived soon enough, not that he was really in the mood for eating anything. His late-night indulgence still reminded him why he didn't partake of whisky on a work night. Elrod Long sat patiently at their designated table in the prison yard, checkerboard set, all to be decided with a coin flip who would make the first move. Elrod had won the toss. Never trust a con man, not even over something a trivial as checkers. Hardy waited for Elrod to bring back up the subject from yesterday, but he never did so he eased into it instead. Hardy Bovine was a *no nonsense*, get straight to the point, don't beat around the bush type guy. He stated it plain and in simple terms, end of story.

He looked Elrod Long dead in the eyes and told him when he died, he had chosen just what his wishes were for having his remains disposed of. Elrod looked a tad bit puzzled, befuddled about the guard's out of nowhere proclamation. Elrod could hardly recall what had happened an hour ago, much less what had happened yesterday. He had no recollection of their previous conversation and just listened as if he were interested in what his checker partner was babbling. Hardy told him he had decided on cremation. Elrod just scratched his ear and nodded. Hardy added that he didn't want his ashes crammed inside a jar or flaunted on s mantle where it would just gather dust. Besides, he had no particular person in mind that would appreciate him resting on their mantle for eternity. Nope, Hardy had something else in mind. It would be something a bit more fitting and fun for everyone but him, since he would be only the source not an active participant. Elrod gave him that *I have no idea what you're talking about* look.

It was simple. Hardy had this little parcel of land over in Summerville, about ten acres to be exact. It was mostly wooded, and he hunted it during the fall, rabbits and squirrels taking up residence, along with deer and a few turkeys. He had once thought about building a cabin on it but never had and likely never would. It was a good hunting spot and a place to just get off to himself and enjoy the peace and quiet of solitude. It was the perfect spot to be put to rest. People who got cremated often wanted their ashes spread someplace. He figured why not him and had the perfect solution for getting it done. He had left explicit instructions, all notarized by Mabel Harrison and documented along with his other important paperwork in his personal records in the prison's human resources department. Hardy told the warden and Human Resources that his close friend, Steele Dillon would be his executor and be allowed access. Steele would be the one to slice open the specially marked envelope in the event he died and there they would find his wishes for being put away along with the cash to do it. He had not told Steele yet though.

After the funeral home cremated him, he wanted his ashes loaded in shotgun shells, however many it took for a man his size. He wanted twelve gage shells used since he owned a double barrel that could be used for the special occasion. He asked that Hubert Wilson, Skipper Pinson and Willy Sprigs all guards, to have the honor of firing his ashes out over his land, or anyone else who wanted to take a shot as far as that goes. Just keep shooting that gun or any other guns until they were plumb out of Hardy Bovine ammunition. Guns and ashes, what a send off fit for a good ole southern boy, that and a final shot each of George Dickel Whisky, green label, 90 proof. No need to BYOB because he was providing the bottle too. Hardy apologized to the inmate, saying he hadn't intentionally excluded him, but they wouldn't allow prisoners to use firearms or drink whiskey, nothing personal, just policy. He smiled and then sincerely thanked the old crusty prisoner for bringing this up yesterday and making him think over just what was the right thing to do for his burial arrangements. Elrod Long looked at the guard real serious like, one of those long and hard stares, before finally speaking his mind, "It's your move but crown me first."

Rectifying a Wrong

Steele Dillon had completed a ten-hour day. Friday had arrived, the end of another work week in the life of a third-generation craftsman. Steele was a master machinist, one of thirteen people employed by McClain's Fabrication and Machine Shop. His father had been a welder and his grandfather, a carpenter. He loved his job, his rural town and life in general. Never married, he lived a private life but did enjoy stopping by the Hiding Hole after work on Fridays for a couple of cold ones and friendly chats with the locals hanging out at the combo bar and grill pool hall. The Hiding Hole was indeed a rundown looking old shack with back country ambiance. It fit his nature like a glove.

Steele had punched the clock, toolbox in one hand and his steel toed workbooks laced and tossed over his shoulder. He had slipped his aching feet into his size fourteen canvas loafers allowing them to breathe a bit. Standing nearly six feet nine and topping three hundred pounds, his feet caught hell standing all day. The parking lot was unusually full for a Friday. His coworkers typically stumbled over one another to exit the premises but not this afternoon for some reason. He shrugged, didn't much matter to him one way or the other, their business, not his.

Something immediately struck him as quite queer. His old truck was not in its usual parking spot. That meant but one thing. Some of the boys were up to one of their stupid ass pranks and he was the target this week. He had grown accustomed to wearing a bull's-eye on his back. Because of his size, men assumed he was a badass. Like how rising gunslingers have this need to challenge the fastest gun, guys perceived him as their ticket to demonstrating just how rough and tough they were. To be the big man they had to beat the biggest man. Steel was not one for fighting. It took a lot to ruffle his feathers to a point he would be forced to defend himself. Friday quitting time wasn't the time to test his patience.

Steele caught glimpses here and there of the other guys straggling behind him. This meant but one thing; they were all in on it. He parked his truck at the far end of the lot to avoid the ruts from the steel delivery trucks. He ignored those who thought they were concealed in their little hiding places and ambled along toward the back lot hopefully to find his truck pushed behind the metal storage shed. It was summer and the windows had been down. Anyone of them could have accessed his truck and taken it out of gear to push it wherever. His was a three on the column, 71 Ford. Steele had restored it to all its glory. He reached a point where he could peek around the building, no truck there. He thought he heard some giggles and muzzled laughs. That meant the truck was close by.

Turning, the temperature in his face rose immediately when he spotted his truck at the bottom of a ten foot ravine, more of a wash near the woods behind the shop. Best he could tell it didn't appear to be harmed. He shook his head though, realizing it was going to be a pain to get it out from down there. He set his shoes and lunchbox down to improve his footing as he half slide, half back crawled down the steep rocky slope. He lost sight of the parking lot as it bottomed out, but he heard the other vehicles cranking and spinning out on the gravel as they exited the premises. Steele interpreted two things from the mass exodus. One, nobody was going to hang around and lay claim to it and secondly, nobody planned to help him get it out.

Steele rubbed his hand alongside the sleekness of the truck as he approached the driver's side door. Reaching for the door handle he pulled it open; not even a squeak as it eased open effortlessly. Inside was a different story. He yelled at the top of his lungs. Riled didn't do his anger justice. The mountain of a man was in full blown fury. They knew what they were doing when they had hauled ass after he vanished down the embankment. Cool, calm, collected no longer described a man who avoided conflict like the plague. He flopped down on the seat and then *two fists* pounded the steering wheel before as quickly as possible scrambling back up the rocky embankment. As expected, the parking lot was empty. McClain had left early as was customary on Fridays to swing by the bank before it closed. That meant Clay Caudal had already locked up. No phone and a long walk were in Steele's Friday afternoon.

****

23

The weekend hadn't passed quickly enough for Steele Dillon. He had managed to repair the damages, but he hadn't managed to control nor quench his temperament. Monday had taken on a whole new meaning this morning, one filled with anticipation and regret, Steele realizing what he must do to make things right for himself and those who had dared do what they had so recklessly done. He had compiled a list of suspects most likely responsible for this, those who thought they had the balls to pull it off. No denying it, all of them were accomplices. One was just as guilty as the next, given the lack of evidence for proving reasonable doubt. He would approach them with this premise in mind.

He punched in, placed his lunch box on the shelf and then sat at his work bench, slipping on and lacing up his work boots. Everything was routine up until now. The shop was empty, but all their vehicles were in the parking lot. He knew where he would find them. All were on the roost, the break room. He wondered what reaction they expected from him. Whatever it was, it was the furthest thing from what they were about to get. Three days they had waited for this and so had he. The wait was over for everyone now. Steele Dillon, more like Marshall Dillon, strolled into the break room, slamming the swinging door aside as if he had just entered the saloon looking for the no-good varmints that had crossed him.

All eyes averted his. Conversations halted. Most were sitting two and three at a table. A couple were standing at the counter near the microwave and coffeepot. Steele commanded the stage and to gain their attention he slammed his open palms loudly atop the first table, the one occupied by Clay Caudal and Rufus Burton. No doubt they had not expected this reaction from the normally meek and mild-mannered Steele Dillon. The fun had quickly deflated from their usual Monday morning banter. They now realized that the big guy didn't appreciate their destructive Friday ruse. Clay managed a quick peek at the mountain standing over them. He remained quiet as a church mouse, as did the others. It was way too late for any of them to back peddle. They were in deep and there was no digging out of this hole.

Steele finally broke the silence. "Morning to all of you. I'm only going to ask this once and expect I know the answer before I ask, but I'm obliged to at least ask. Who schemed and perpetrated Friday's hateful and spiteful vandalism?"

The break room remained deathly silent. Most were staring into space or at their feet or coffee mugs. No one looked in Steele's direction

"As I had figured. So be it then. Albert, Stub, please have a seat. It's funny, usually the alleged defendant's fate rests on the twelve jurors of his or her peers slated to determine if they are innocent or guilty of the crime presented. It seems we have a reversal of roles in this case. I stand here before you, twelve defendants, as the 'all inclusive', one-man jury, prosecutor and judge. Thank you for assembling in this break room, your trial room, your courthouse and where punishment shall be decided and delivered, if you are found guilty of the crime as presented shortly."

The room remained deathly quiet. His coworkers knew him as mild mannered, a person of very few words, a get it done type and not one to be boisterous nor confrontational. That was the side he had allowed them to see. Up until now Steele had kept it in check but that was before they had messed with his truck. Today he would let it fly and unleash the inner angry side. Not his fault, it was on them.

"As prosecutor of this travesty, I now present the case against the defendants. Exhibit one." Steele then tossed a series of photographs onto the table, photos of the interior of his truck taken from several angles. He motioned for Clay and Rufus to pass them around.

"The 1971 Ford pickup in those photos, my truck was located at the bottom of the gully behind McClain's Fabrication and Machine Shop. You will notice that the turn signal lever and the gearshift are missing, snapped off, not merely removed. Three on a tree has been lost in translation. The owner of said truck in the photos had to walk four miles to then make a phone call for a tow truck. I present exhibit B, the receipt for that towing charge. While I am at, here's exhibit C, the receipt to replace the parts to repair the truck's damages. Labor has been factored into that cost. Any questions so far? I didn't think so. As prosecutor it is my obligation to offer a plea deal for those willing to accept responsibility for their actions. I must communicate to you though that there are twelve allegedly accused perpetrators of this crime; however, it is the belief of the court that it was planned by a mere few. This doesn't absolve those who had knowledge of the crime; one for all, live by the sword, die by the sword."

A few squirmed but nobody took the bait or the deal.

"I think we can dispense with the normal proceedings. We could just step outside and settle this like men, but you boys are far from that, low life that you are. Let's face facts. None of you can take me in a fair or unfair fight. It would be an old fashion ass whooping for all of you and it would rob me of the satisfaction of knowing who did this and why. No. I've got another way to achieve my goal in mind."

Clay finally spoke up, "Come on Steele, enough's enough. You have made your point. The Bossman isn't going to take it too lightly you keeping us from working and all."

"Bossman is not here. I met him in the drive as I pulled in. He's off to quote a job. He told me that Betsy won't be in today either. One of her kids is sick and can't attend school. Nobody is in the office either. It appears we have plenty of time to complete this trial after all."

Clay stood as did Conner, Mark, Ray and Wylie. Steele pushed back his coat to reveal the handgun resting in his belt.

"Don't do something stupid, Steele," warned Clay.

"Beyond stupid commenced Friday afternoon. Have a seat, boys. Court isn't adjourned just yet. We're going to deviate from the normal process. I believe I can speed up things and narrow the field of those responsible for perpetrating the most heinous crime on my truck."

With that, Steele retrieved the revolver from his belt, opened then spun the cylinder, emptying the six bullets into his palm. He then as quickly, loaded one bullet back in the cylinder, spun it and closed it.

"There are five empty slots and twelve of you with only six playing the first round. Those six will be Rufus, Coy, Conner, Tad, Wylie, Keith and you, Clay. Each takes a turn and if you're lucky you have a chance to witness the luck of the next participant. This ends when I have a confession, a full confession. Who orchestrated Friday's destruction of my Ford and who actively participated? The remainder of you boys don't get off Scott-free because you were accessories to the fact and knew exactly what was being perpetrated. I take that into account when I divvy out the just punishment."

"This is crazy, Steele. It will justify you being fired and arrested," warned Clay.

"Perhaps you'd like to go first Clay. I didn't think so."

Steele placed the barrel of his gun against Coy's forehead, finger resting on the trigger. "Now Coy Newton, you are aware of the crimes committed. Do you have anything to say before we continue what might persuade the jury to rethink its verdict and have mercy on your sorry soul?"

"It was Coot and Bartley that did it. None of the rest of us had anything to do with it."

"But all of you knew it, didn't you?"

He nodded yes.

"And Clay, you were the foreman in charge and did nothing to stop it, did you?"

"I didn't know they were going to damage your truck. They were just supposed to roll it to the bottom. That's all."

"Shut the hell up, Clay," shouted Barkley. "You knew exactly what was being done. It was your idea. You said you wanted to fix his ass. He was the Bossman's favorite, and you were tired of playing second fiddle to him."

"That's right, Steele blame Clay. He hates your guts, always has. He felt threatened and wanted to teach you a lesson. He paid us good to do it. Just being the shop foreman wasn't enough for him."

"And the rest of you did absolutely nothing, fearful of losing your jobs, I suppose. How long have I known you boys? We've never had any disagreements or harsh words. Why would you conspire to do this and go along with Clay? That's mighty hurtful and a bit much to swallow to just let it go."

"Steele, you better put down that gun, boy," advised Clay.

"I suppose you're right, Clay. I shouldn't be poking it against poor Coy's head. I might accidentally get a little trigger happy." Steele then removed the barrel from Coy and placed it against Clay's head instead.

"You've proved your silly ass point, Steele. You best put that thing away before you do more harm."

"Hold on a second, Clay. The jury hasn't delivered their verdict yet. What say the jury, Mister Foreman? Guilty you say. Judge and what is the sentence for the crimes committed by Clay Caudal? Death, you say and no appeal."

Coot jumped in, "This is a crock of crap, and you know it, Steele. Bossman will have your ass for what you have done, and the sheriff is going to lock your butt up and toss away the key. This has worked out better than I could have ever imagined it."

"Choices, Clay and you have two. Step outside and take an ass whooping like you have never had or I can pull this trigger and we can see just how your luck plays out. You pick or I will."

"Screw you, Steele. Big man and all mouth! You're just a big ole wussie and always have been. It'll tickle me to death to see you locked up and out of here."

"Death, you say," and with that, Steele pulled the trigger.

'Click', everyone cringed.

"Bastard," mouthed Clay.

Steele pulled the trigger again… 'Click' and then again, 'Click', and then a fourth and fifth, 'Click, Click.' Clay had already pissed his pants and was lightheaded and weak kneed.

Steele smiled, "One left, boy, justice served." He pulled the trigger. Clay fell backwards over his chair. 'Click.'

"No live ammo necessary for a confession so it seems."

He just as quickly sprung back to his feet, chair in hand, swinging wildly at Steele. Steele caught the chair with one hand and Clay by the shirt with the other. He snatched the chair from Clay and delivered a right fist to Clay's jaw, sending him flying across the break room and into the counter. The coffee pot landed and broke over his head.

Red McClain stepped though the doorway. Clay shaking the cobwebs, tried to stand, pointing at Steele and muttering something as he spat blood and broken teeth from his mouth.

"You're fired son and don't try to pull anything foolish against anyone here or my company. Every man in this room will back me up or collect their last paycheck. You started it, enough said. Collect your belongings and get the hell out of here, Clay. Sorry, Steele, this should have never happened. Coot, Barkley, you are fired too. Your last paychecks go to Steele as restitution for repairs to his truck, the wrecker bill and the anguish he suffered. I'd suggest you consider relocating out of this county. Word spreads fast where backstabbing and disloyalty is concerned. Thank you for filling me in Steele. This was a fine plan you concocted to smoke out the low life that perpetrated it and rectify the wrong done to you and your vehicle. By the way, congratulations; you're the new shop foreman. Boys, you're on the clock and work won't get done from this break room. Not a word of what happened Friday or today if you still cherish having a job here or anyplace else in the county. Do I make myself perfectly clear? And consider yourselves lucky that I didn't allow Mister Dillon to square things with all of you. Be sure to thank him too. As a favor to him, you still have your jobs. He's a better man than me."

"Thank you, Mr. McClain," said Steele offering his hand.

Accepting the handshake, he replied, "It's Red, and I'll expect to see you at supper tonight. We have a lot to discuss about our shop and me planning that early retirement next year."

Knight Moves

Eddy Southard stared at the wall clock, the minute hand traveling a bit slow for his liking. There were no customers in the store and Wednesdays the town rolled up its sidewalks with most establishments closing at noon. Such was the way it had always been. Eddy wasn't sure how the tradition had started nor why it was still practiced. It didn't much matter to him, getting a half day off and all. Old man Jenkins always left it up to him to close up the hardware shop on Wednesdays. Eddy was only sixteen, but Jenkins considered him to be a responsible teenager. He even trusted him with handling the money and dropping it by the bank. Not bad for a part timer and a kid as perceived by most. It was a summer job until school started. Well part time was anyone's interpretation. He worked weekdays and Saturday right now. When school was back in session, he would only work Saturdays. His folks would not allow him to work after school.

After closing he had one delivery to make before he headed over to Pop's County One Stop. Hardy Bovine had placed an order for a roll of chicken wire and metal posts. Jenkins allowed him to use the store's pickup. Hardy Bovine would not be home yet, but he had told him ahead of time where to place the goods. Sweat dripped off his nose and beaded on his forehead as he loaded the wire and posts. Eddie pushed his black wire rim glasses back in place after they had shifted on his nose. He liked Mister Hardy and enjoyed the prison stories he shared with him. That man could tell some wild ones. Fact, Eddy enjoyed hanging out with older folks more than he did those his own age. Other kids did not get him. He worked while they got into mischief and had fun, feeling their oats and enjoying their teenage lives. Eddy didn't get them either, not that it bothered him much one way or the other. Some said he was cheating his youth. Eddy didn't feel like a cheater and what some said did not hold water as for as he was concerned.

It was a short distance to Mister Hardy's by the way the crow flies, a lot further taking the road route. The old man treasured his privacy.

His place was secluded and off the beaten path for sure. Eddy wondered if he had plans for raising chickens given the manifesto of the delivery. Mister Hardy did not seem to be the chicken raising type especially given the hours he still worked at the prison. It was none of his business whatever plans he had for the wire and metal poles. Knowing Mister Hardy, he would probably share his reasons for it sooner or later. He liked to talk more than he liked keeping secrets. He would often say how he was an open book, too old to play hide and seek and worry about what others thought about him and his ways. Straight shooting took the crooked roads out of play was the way he saw it. Odd saying but he had a knack for putting his unique spin on almost any situation.

The turn off to his driveway was ahead. Unmarked it was easy to miss if you didn't know it was there. There was no mailbox. Not that he did not trust the mail carries, he just didn't trust people meddling in his business, taking stuff from the mailbox that didn't belong to them. Eddy suspected he had one of those post office boxes but he never mentioned having one and Eddy never asked. He had no reason to question how he got his mail. He simply respected Mister Hardy's business and any quirkiness that went along with it. Eddy had his fair share of quirkiness and understood the boundaries that went along with it.

He kicked up a dust storm behind him as he drove down the dirt road to his house. Tall pines anchored both sides of the drive, so thick they seemed impenetrable. He figured this was by design offering more seclusion to his reclusive lifestyle. It was odd, a man who worked in the public's eye doing the opposite when off the clock. It was almost as if he preferred being imprisoned both at work and at home. No, imprisoned at home was not a proper analogy. Privacy yes but not imprisoned. Reaching the break in the trees Eddy wheeled the pickup to the shed where he had been instructed to unload the goods. If he had not been here so many times it might have felt a bit too secluded and spooky. It didn't though. He felt as much at home as he did anywhere. He spent plenty of time on that front porch rocking and chewing the fat with Mister Hardy. Good times indeed, the best memories for sure in his young life. Thinking, talking and playing checkers were always part of the agenda.

After unloading the truck, he headed to Pop's Country One Stop. There he would have his usual special, two hotdogs all the way, a bag of Fritos and a Dr. Pepper. The One Stop had a huge porch out front, thus earning the country part of its name. It more resembled an old country store than a run of the mill 7-Eleven convenience store. Like Mister Hardy's, it had several rockers out front, and a table set with a checkerboard. If he was lucky there would be someone there itching for a friendly game of checkers. If not, he would just enjoy his special and top it off with an ice cream sandwich. Nope, he was not squandering his youth. not by a long shot. It didn't get much better than the life he had chosen to live. It suited him just fine, doing it his way just like Mister Hardy had taught him to do. Live your life and be happy as best you can he would say adding that you are riding in the front seat, but the Lord is always behind the wheel.

Eddy entered the store and spotted a familiar face at the checkout. Steele Dillon had probably just gotten off work from McClain's Machine Shop. If anyone visited Mister Hardy more than him it had to be Steele Dillon. Mister Hardy said kindred spirits were drawn to one another like kids to candy. Eddy felt blessed and comfortable belonging to this kindred spiritual circle even with the generational gaps that existed. Steele gathered his bag and turned spotting him. A large smile broke out on his face.

"Eddy, here for your usual like me, two all the way, chips and a soda?"

"You got it Steele and looking for a checker game."

"Love to take you up on it but it was a long day at the shop, short handed," but Steel did not fill Eddy in on the reason behind being short handed, the firing of those that had dared damage his truck and the lack of productivity by the coconspirators impacted by his actions this morning to flush out the perpetrators. The outcome could have been worse for those involved. They could have been fired too or taken out back to the woodshed by him.

"Maybe next time then," Eddy replied. "Are you heading out to Mister Hardy's Saturday?"

"I would never pass up a fish fry. What about you?"

"I have already asked off work. I can hardly wait."

"See you there then Eddy. Hope you find your checker game," said Steele as he gave him a friendly pat on the back when passing.

Eddy stepped up to the counter and placed his order. While waiting, his mind pondered the mystery behind his favorite store. Oddly there was no Pop or male associated with Pop's Country One Stop. Geneva Abbott was the only owner and operator of the country store. Some thought she had named it Pop's because of the rural setting that catered to hunters, fishermen and truckers. That made no sense to Eddy. Plenty of places were named after women. Why not Geneva's or Abbott's Country One Stop instead. After all, the hotdog chili recipe was supposed to be hers, something secretive like Colonel Sander's KFC. Kellie served up his meal with a friendly smile making him forget about what he was thinking. He was a bit smitten by her, but she barely noticed him. She was two years older and had a thing for jocks. He was the furthest thing from being a jock, end of that fantasy.

Out on the porch he staked out the table with the checkerboard and scoffed down his two hotdogs then casually munched on the corn chips while finishing off his Dr. Pepper. Eddy then set up the checkerboard hopeful someone would drop by and take him up a friendly game. It wasn't looking too likely though, most just gassing up and going on their way. The rumbling engine and screeching brakes caught his attention. A Greyhound Bus pulled to a stop out front. This was not a typical bus stop, well out of the way for most bus routes. Steam hissing and rising from the engine tipped him off that this was not a scheduled stop. He overheard the driver asking Bud Sellers if there was a garage with a mechanic on duty nearby that could replace a ruptured radiator hose. The nearest was at least thirty minutes from the store.

There was nothing to do but offload the passengers for a spell while the driver hitched a ride with Bud to the repair shop. Seven people exited the bus. One man was livid and cursing up a storm. A young couple didn't seem to mind and decided to take a stroll. A lady with three children went inside. Another man settled in on the porch planting his butt in a rocker. He seemed a bit perturbed too but let out no rants like the other guy. After a spell the man eased from his rocker and walked over to where Eddy sat in front of the checkerboard.

"Mind if I have a seat young man?"

Eddy offered him a courtesy shrug.

"Checkers…"

"Yep, do you play?"

"Did you know there is another game played on this board?"

Eddy shrugged again and asked, "Do you want to play a game of checkers?"

"What would you say to us playing a game of chess?"

"I don't know how to play chess. Besides, I don't have any chess pieces, just checkers."

"Have you ever played chess young man?"

"Just checkers."

"Would you like to learn the gentleman's game of chess?"

"Like I said, don't have any chess pieces."

"Excuse me. I shall return."

Eddy watched him as he exited the porch and climbed on board the bus. The gentleman was decked out in tweed, a brown jacket, matching vest and pants, white shirt and red tie. He seemed a bit over dressed to be traveling by Greyhound but what did Eddy know about how bus passengers were supposed to dress. He watched and waited. A few minutes later he retuned carrying a leather case. He then set it on the table and opened it.

"We have chess pieces, House of Staunton, 40,000-year-old wooly mammoth to be specific. Allow me to show you how to set the board. I shall do the blacks and you mirror your side of the board with the white pieces. Pardon my rudeness, might I inquire whom I shall be mentoring?'

"Eddy Southard."

"Splendid, Edward, pleasure to make your acquaintance. You may address me as Luigi, incognito traveling this quaint countryside via that abomination. Price one must endure to travel anonymously."

Eddy did not know how to respond so he didn't. Apparently, this Luigi feller thought he should recognize him, but he had never met anyone who played chess. He replicated Luigi's placement of the chess pieces on his side of the board. This was a far cry from checkers. His mentor, as he referred to himself, proceeded in naming each piece and explaining how they could move on the board, what the various pieces could do and what they couldn't do. Complicated didn't begin to address the challenges. Unlike checkers, jumping a piece to take it, there was only one piece that could jump others and mere jumping did not remove pieces from the board. The horse or knight as he called it could move three positions, twice in the same direction and then one square sideways. When the knight landed on the space with an opposing piece that piece was removed from the board. Rooks and bishops could travel uniquely about the board. The queen was the only piece besides the king that could move in any direction. The pawns seemed to be tokens unless one made it across the length of the board where it could be swapped for any piece except the king. Already Eddy's head felt woozy with what Luigi was tossing at him. The objective was to checkmate the king and say checkmate when you succeeded.

36

Luigi watched patiently as his young protégé mastered the various moves of each piece. He was amazed at how quickly Edward had grasped the concept of the game. Once he sensed the lad was comfortable, he announced, "Shall we have a go?" Eddy confirmed with a nod and made his first move, white king's pawn e2 to e4. Luigi countered, more mesmerized by the twinkle in Edward's eyes. Edward moved his white king's bishop f1 to c4. Without given the lad's move much thought, Luigi countered all the while focused on Edward instead of the board. Third move, white queen d1 to h5 and Luigi sensed something but reacted indifferently with a nonchalant counter. Next move, Eddy quickly maneuvered his white queen to take the black f7 claiming checkmate.

"Impossible! Scholars Mate, four moves, how could you have possibly defeated me with Scholars Mate?"

Eddy shrugged. "It is checkmate, isn't it?'

"And you have never played chess?"

"Never until now," replied Eddy.

"I am a GM."

"A what," inquired Eddy.

"Grand Master and you are certainly incapable of defeating a GM. I am mere months away from challenging the reigning world champion. Do you realize how this will tarnish my reputation?"

"So, I didn't win then?"

"Scholars Mate, amateurish," fumed Luigi.

"I get it. I am an amateur, but you are the one who wanted to teach me how to play chess. I was perfectly fine with playing checkers."

Luigi quickly packed his chess set back inside the leather case. Eddy eyed his pale pasty white face, the alleged chess grandmaster flabbergasted after the sudden defeat. Unfazed by what had happened, Eddy asked, "Would you like to play a game of checkers now? The bus driver isn't back yet."

Luigi offered no response. He simply exited the porch and returned to the bus with not so much as a goodbye. Kellie slipped outside for a smoke but had seen the man's odd actions.

"What's got his panties in a wad?"

"The feller sure takes his chess seriously. I never saw such a bad loser other than Roger Argo when I beat him at checkers four times in a row. You would think he would be proud that he taught me how to play and I won my first time trying. Boring game if you ask me, over just like that with all those pieces still left on the board."

"I wouldn't take it so hard, Eddy. Winners are always better than sorry losers in my book. You care for a victory smoke?"

"Thanks, but no thanks, I should be heading home."

"Suit yourself, congrats on your chess victory."

"Whoop dido, I am the champion of my world I suppose. See you later, Kellie."

"Don't do anything I wouldn't, Eddy."

Fat chance thought Eddy.

"Hey Lover Boy, how are they hanging?"

Eddy looked over at the gas pumps and replied, "I learned to play chess a while ago."

Sookie Cantrell straddled her 1984 Harley Softail, decked out in leather from head to foot. The black boisterous and bosomy biker, a tall drink of water she was, resembled an Amazon warrior. She towered over Eddy by at least four inches, and he was a slender toothpick of almost five eleven. Sookie embraced the roadways. Her only transportation year-round was her Softail. She could put the postal service to shame with her rain, sleet or snow approach to delivering the goods. Sookie lived by the mantra *some will walk through the Pearly Gates and some will ride.* No one embraced the saying more *it takes more love to share the saddle than it does to share the sheets.* To call her a unique person was highly understated. Tough as nails on the outside she had a heart of gold on the inside.

"Chess huh, you are the ultimate brainiac. Not surprised."

"Are you going to Mister Hardy's fish fry Saturday?"

"Invite confirmed. Wouldn't miss the special camaraderie it offers, peas in a pod for the shelling. Do you need a ride?"

"Thanks, but I have Jenkin's pickup. I made a delivery out at Mister Hardy's place earlier, but he was not home. Where are you heading?"

"Like they say, you don't always need a plan, just go. Me, I just need a Harley between my legs and the lust to ride. See you Saturday Lover Boy."

She smiled as she mounted her Harley, thinking how Eddy called her Sookie out in public. It was expected she supposed. She was the infamous Sookie, reputation earned for those visualizing her as someone she wasn't. Among real friends away from the scrutiny of everyday life she was anybody but Sookie. She enjoyed her life as Sookie but loved her life of less notoriety more.

Got My Motor Runnin'

Susan Cantrell lived the dream, free spirited and uninhibited. Harley Davidson set in motion her transformation when she was just nineteen. Lost souls need something to latch onto if ever they hope to navigate what the world tosses their way. Frank 'Crawdaddy' Crawford paved the way for the girl floundering in turbulent waters. He saw her potential and gambled on mentoring her and utilizing the skills his gut told him that she had hemmed up inside. Crawdaddy owned the local Harley Davidson Shop. He noticed the gleam in Susan's eyes every time she visited the shop with her cousin Howie Buzhardt, proud owner of a 250 Harley dirt bike.

While at the shop she hung on every word the repairman tossed out as he discussed mechanical and electrical diagnosed options for various customers seeking answers for their bike's woes. She often jumped in sleeves rolled up to assist, more of a gopher for Wiley at first handing the repairman whatever tool he needed. Initially she could not identify them, but she quickly caught on and began coming by and hanging out at the shop without her cousin. Crawdaddy did not discourage her even though some of the patrons of the shop did not appreciate a female hanging out in what they considered the 'all men's club.' Their opinion, females were biker chicks, mere riders and never the operators of the bike. Crawdaddy scolded those who openly shared their biased opinions in the presence of his young apprentice.

Soon Susan had earned the respect of many of those that had once shunned her. She had a gift for trouble shooting and could usually figure out any bike problem and fix it. Crawdaddy and his resident mechanic, Wiley Fritz, taught her what she didn't know or struggled to understand. Eventually she could tear down a bike and reassemble it making it better than new. Customers came in specifically asking for Sue to diagnose their problems. Wiley beamed with delight watching her work her magic like an old pro. Crawdaddy asked her if she had ever thought about riding. She had but said she could not afford a bike. Crawdaddy smiled and told her to follow him. He directed her to a Harley, a rusty Softail frame and said have at it,

40

pointing to shelves of spare parts. Susan looked at him puzzled. He made it simple for her to understand. You build it from scratch, and you own it, adding 'show me what you can do.' He noticed that familiar sparkle in her eyes, the one that inspired him to give her a try in the first place.

Susan embraced the opportunity wholeheartedly. She mesmerized Crawdaddy with her tenacity and determination. Crawdaddy instructed Wiley to stay out of it and allow her to work through it and make her own mistakes; only intervene if she asked and even then, instruct her and refrain from doing it for her. This was her build, plain and simple. Susan seldom asked for help but when she did it was usually something well above her pay grade and experience. With a few basic instructions she would be back on tract and on her own once again. She was a relentless hellfire, often working well past midnight. Crawdaddy just asked her to set the alarm and lock up, giving her free reigns.

In a little over three weeks, she had completed her masterpiece. She would have been finished within hours had she had new parts available. Much time was spent refurbishing used parts available. Crawdaddy told her everything she needed was in the salvage area. All she had to do was locate them and make them new again. He pushed back on ordering her any parts, assured that everything needed could be found if she looked hard enough. This was as much a final examine as it was for her personal benefit. If she passed with flying colors, she would also be the proud owner of a Harley. If she passed, he would be offering her a fulltime job. He never doubted that she would succeed. Wiley also beamed with pride and never considered her a threat to his continued employment. There was plenty of work to go around with the growing business, especially with the focus shifting to new custom builds.

Judgment day arrived. Her Harley was ready for the ultimate test, firing it up. Many of the regulars had heard about what she had been doing and dropped by frequently to quiz Wiley or Crawdaddy on her progress. Even though today was not perceived as a reveal plenty of folks showed up at the shop to be part of the unscheduled event. Susan, while nervous, welcomed one and all, proud of her accomplishment no matter how it turned out. Hoyt Cranston even offered her a ceremonious drum roll on an oil drum as she prepared to kick start her creation. The Harley fired up on the first attempt to the claps, hoots and hollers of those inside the shop. Wiley handed her a new helmet he had bought for her and then encouraged her to take it for a spin. She did, storming out of the shop and up the road again to the cheers of those there to witness her accomplishment.

Frank 'Crawdaddy' Crawford was especially beaming with delight like a proud papa. She had passed with flying colors just like he had expected her to do. That girl had something special he would often tell Wiley, the uncanny ability when it came to motorcycle repairs. Crawdaddy had shared with Wiley his intent to hire her, and he had told his boss that it was a smart move before someone else scooped her up. Her reputation had already created interest from several other bike businesses in surrounding counties. A newspaper reporter had wanted to cover the event, but Crawdaddy had pushed back on that saying it would be her decision afterwards if she wished to talk to him. The publicly would be good either way but he just wanted it for Susan. Business was good without it.

Wiley had prepared something a little extra for her return to the shop. Hoyt was on lookout, but it wasn't necessary. Everyone could hear her approaching, the sounds of the engine music to their ears. He waited until she pulled inside the shop and shut off the engine before springing his little surprise, a fitting tribute to her and her accomplishments. He switched on the boom box and let it fly, a Steppenwolf classic 'Sookie Sookie'.

Let it hang out baby, let it hang out now, now na-na now
Let it hang out baby, everybody work out
Sookie, Sookie, Sookie, Sookie, Sookie, Sookie, Sue

Let it hang out baby, do the Baltimore jig
Let it hang out baby, boomerang with me
Sookie, Sookie, Sookie, Sookie, Sookie, Sookie, Sue

Really got it bad child, drink a bottle of turpentine
When you wake up in the morning, feelin' kinda fine

Let it hang out baby, let it hang out now, now na-na now

You better watch your step girl, don't step on that banana peel
If your foot should ever hit it, you'll go up to the ceiling
Hang it in baby, hang it in baby
Sookie, Sookie, Sookie, Sookie, Sookie, Sookie, Sue

Let it hang out baby, let it hang out now, now na-na now
Let it hang out baby, everybody work out
Hang it in baby, hang it in baby, hang it in baby
Sookie, Sookie, Sookie, Sookie, Sookie, Sookie, Sue

Whoops and howls almost drowned out the song lyrics, a fitting tribute indeed to a lady that had surpassed expectations. It didn't take long for the crowd to begin chanting 'Sookie, Sookie, Sue.' Thereafter, Susan 'Sue' Cantrell had earned her nickname 'Sookie'. Forever Sookie she would be, and she embraced her newfound namesake and loyal following, humbled by the experience. Once the shop had cleared Crawdaddy pulled her aside and offered her a fulltime position. Wiley winked and nodded his approval.

Crawdaddy years later made twenty-seven-year-old Sookie a partner in the business. He had been pushing back from the everyday activities and primarily focused on keeping the books and managing the payroll. She ran the shop, ordered parts and oversaw all rebuilds. She had two mechanics working for her, one seasoned and the other a newbie learning the ropes. Sadly, Wiley had died two years prior, victim of a tragic accident. His sidecar had been broadsided by motorist distracted while texting. Wiley had been pronounced dead at the scene. In memory at his funeral a local band had preformed one of Wiley's favorite songs; Steppenwolf's 'Born to be Wild'. Those in attendance belted out the lyrics loudly and proudly. It had been a perfect last tribute.

Get your motor runnin'
Head out on the highway
Lookin' for adventure
And whatever comes our way

Yeah Darlin' go make it happen
Take the world in a love embrace
Fire all of your guns at once
And explode into space

I like smoke and lightning
Heavy metal thunder
Racin' with the wind
And the feelin' that I'm under

Yeah Darlin' go make it happen
Take the world in a love embrace
Fire all of your guns at once
And explode into space

Like a true nature's child
We were born, born to be wild
We can climb so high
I never wanna die

Born to be wild
Born to be wild

One year after his death Sookie had founded a Motorcycle Club in his memory. Membership had skyrocketed immediately for the newly formed Wiley Riders MC. Sookie, a woman blazing the trail had attracted more women riders, their numbers rivaling their male counterparts within the club.

It was after forming the club that she had first met Steele Dillon. They were sponsoring a toy ride to benefit orphan children at the Britton Center Orphanage when Steele heard about it and stepped up to make a generous donation. She and Steele had hit it off immediately. He was one of integrity who had a soft spot for those less fortunate in this world. The next year Steele had gotten McClain's Fabrication and Machine Shop to be a huge sponsor of the toy ride. Also tossing in a generous donation had been a man named Hardy Bovine, Steele's friend. Sookie met Hardy for the first time at the event held at the Britton Center. The three ironically developed an unlikely bond given their diverse backgrounds. No doubting it though, once the friendship had been firmly established, each would forever have the other's backs though thick and thin.

Sookie, now twenty-nine with two years under her belt at Crawdaddy's still missed her mentor, Wiley. She owned three motorcycles, all Harleys, and one of her favorites was the sidecar previously ridden by Wiley that she had salvaged from that terrible accident. After topping off her tank at Pop's Country One Stop she had ridden past the spot where Wiley had lost his life. She rode this route often, sometimes stopping and talking to Wiley, telling him how much she missed him. One valuable lesson she learned from his untimely death, never text or talk on a cell phone while driving or riding any vehicle. She and Crawdaddy had sponsored an annual charity event to honor Wiley and support an organization for vehicular awareness, stressing the importance of focusing on the road, not everything otherwise while operating cars, trucks and motorcycles. She looked forward to the upcoming fish fry out at Hardy's place. The love and fellowship would be a welcome change given recent circumstances that had reared its ugly head in her life. She had long ago put the past in her rearview mirror or so she thought. Why now? Why ever?

A Closet Filled with Skeletons and Kitty Cats

Hardy Bovine wasn't without skeletons in his family closet. He dwelled on this too often for his liking. The recent revelations and funeral preparation brainstorming had brought them back to light once again. A man living by his lonesome has way too much time on his hands. Digging up long buried bones tends to come naturally whether you embrace them or not. Hardy's brain literally had a mind of its own. It sounded just plain silly, him having such a crazy perception of what was inside his head and what made it go rogue when it decided to dig up stuff it had no business excavating. Yet here I am he thought, at its mercy whether I like it or not. And like it he didn't. He figured he should be the one in control and not tainted memories that had no business surfacing out of nowhere. Once those skeletons from the past were out of the closet any argument and protest launched by him was futile at best. Might as well just get it over and let it run its course. Not that he had choice, it was time to pour a drink or five to try to deaden the pain surely heading his way. There was nothing worse than relatives that tarnished the family name.

His Uncle Tom had brought shame to the family a few years back, the long arm of the law reeling him in like a floundering and flopping hooked catfish. It was regretful to think of his kin this way because he had always been sort of fond of Uncle Tom, his mother's brother. He still was but just kept those feelings buried and out of the public's eye. He certainly hadn't shared Uncle Tom's legacy with any prison folks. Uncle Tom had been owner of an antiquated funeral parlor. Hardy had even worked there a time or two back in his younger days but never hankered to be a mortician, not that he didn't have the stomach for it. He hadn't grown up with that many friends to start with, but no one liked hanging out with an undertaker unless they were creepy too. Uncle Tom had a little sideline going, an illegal tattoo parlor in the basement of his funeral home. His downfall had come when he screwed up the tattoos of Councilman Porter Brooks' six granddaughters. Honest mistakes can happen. They had wanted their names tattooed on their left shoulders. Hard of hearing, Uncle Tom had tattooed *Prunes* on their shoulders, each lined up like cordwood, none seeing the final masterpiece until the last girl had been marked. Their last name was *Trunes*. The poor girls could no longer go to the public swimming pool without drawing out bullying and loud laughter.

One thing led to another. The local law enforcement investigated and discovered his little illegal sideline. Worse still, they uncovered an even darker secret with his entrepreneurship. It seems that old Uncle Tom had been utilizing the byproduct from his crematorium in his resourceful operation. The deceased's ashes were being blended with tattoo ink, an obvious cost savings for Uncle Tom, bargain basement prices he passed on to his clients. Not everyone was pleased to hear they were sporting cadavers, some that they even knew, in their tattoos. Nope, sometimes you've got to keep things like this close to the vest. Even though his uncle had served less than a year, time served and good behavior, it's not something that you'd want to be associated with. It was worse than being an undertaker or an undertaker's gopher. Hardy was glad he had never had a wild hair about getting a tattoo. Uncle Tom had offered to give him the family discount on numerous occasions. Poor old Uncle Tom had died two years ago after consuming a fruit salad over at Carver's Bait and Tackle, Gas and Go Deli. The new cook there had used chopped up prunes in the salad, unaware that Uncle Tom was highly allergic to them. He had swollen up like a bullfrog, his tongue choking off his oxygen intake. Justice can be served in the strangest ways, so said the Trunes sisters.

Hardy Bovine was startled, and he didn't startle easily, by Clabber rubbing between his legs. Clabber was one of two cats he owned. Well, maybe they owned him. He didn't like cats or hadn't until he found a litter of three tied in a burlap croaker sack in the dumpster. Two had been a dirty white color and the third a calico, a very dead calico. The kittens had been abandoned and mostl likely left for dead. For one out of three the scheme had worked. He should have minded in his own business and left well enough alone. Hardy hadn't needed any scrawny flea-bitten kittens complicating his uncomplicated life. The pathetic meowing had been difficult to ignore, and he had honestly tried to walk away. On impulse, he retrieved and untied the sack, intent on just setting them free. Stupid

47

ass kittens, you have to feed them and tend to them. He had named the other one Buttermilk after burying their brother, which he didn't name. Buttermilk perched on the back of the couch, her usual napping spot in front of the window. The sisters were now three years old. What had he been thinking? He went to the pantry and then refilled their food bowl, reaching down to give each a little rub, damn *good for nothing* cats.

Dogs were a better fit for a man, but he wasn't particularly fond of dogs either. He really wasn't an animal person unless they were critters he could cook and eat. Cats were not appealing to his appetite although he had heard rumors about a local Asian restaurant located next door to a veterinarian. Rumors surfaced a while back that they had a little arrangement that involved a beneficial disposal process for deceased animals. Thankfully, Asian cuisine was not Hardy's cup of tea. He had gotten his fill of it while serving as an Army Ranger overseas during the WWII. He had sworn off it once his toes touched American soil upon his return stateside.

Another dark blemish on the family tree had been loony cousin Rockwell Bovine, a self-made iron chef. Rocky was no more of an iron chef than Hardy was a famous cast iron skillet chef. Rocky dabbled in off the way food preparation. Hardy would normally eat anything that did not eat him first, but he did not trust Rocky and his off the wall recipes. Rocky would give them unique names but would never share what ingredients were used for his concoctions. Hardy would try anything provided he knew what he was trying. Something smelled literally when it came to what Rocky was serving on his menu. Having a vet less than a block away raised a bit of suspicion. Perin Paulson who operated the local and only grocery nearby often commented that Rocky seldom purchased any meats from him. This did not add up when you perused the menu where Rocky worked. Meat was included in any dish, and he was the one responsible for making purchases. It was rumored that Rocky was pocketing the money that he was supposed to use for these purchases. Do the math, so said Hardy. More ugly skeletons in the family closet that he did his best not to claim. He eyed Buttermilk and Clabber, visions he would just as soon get out of his head.

You can pick your friends but not your family. You can un-friend a friend and disown a family member. Friends might buy into this arrangement, but family are still kin no matter what. No denying it, the Bovines were a quirky and unique bunch that Hardy was stuck with whether he liked it or not. Hardy wasn't ashamed of any of his kin like most might be, he just viewed them as stains nothing more. Growing up around the challenged kinfolks distorted his view of them as a chap. So much exposure to abnormal seemed perfectly normal. Even Aunt Cora had her moments memorable even to this very day. Hardy could smell those distinctive odors of her house when he thought about her. Some houses are musty while others permeate of home cooking or baked goods. Not Aunt Cora's. Multiple his two cats by a zillion, so it seemed back then, gave it a distinctive feline stench. Cat hair and cat poop were in no short supply. Thinking back on it now, Hardy identified the reason he hated cats. It was deep seeded in his childhood memories. Most visitors, friends and family pushed back on Aunt Cora's invites to dine there.

Hardy as a little chap was terrified by the assortment of cats, many being feral for sure. Aunt Cora with her open door turned away no cat. She couldn't have even if she had wanted to during warm weather. Her screen door had a gaping hole clawed clean through it offering free reign in and out. Other critters took to her hospitality and open-door policy. Hardy had seen raccoons and possums among the cats. They say if you have cats around, your house and barn are usually free from mice and rats. Hardy could never remember ever seeing a mouse, a rat, a squirrel or rabbit on her property. Cora the cat lady's reputation lived large in the rural community. Hardy tried as best he could to get out of visits, his mama dragging him along. Aunt Cora was her sister, blood kin trumping cat clutter every time. He never heard Ruth, his mama, ever say a single bad thing about her sister. He never witnessed her eat anything there either. Hardy wandered back outside once the greetings and hugs were over. Even out there did not grant total reprieve from cat world. Cats tend to follow you about meowing and rubbing against you. He wasn't sure if the cats were trying to be friendly or were just hungry. He wasn't absolutely convinced that a herd of them couldn't overtake him. He learned quickly that you cannot climb something to escape cats.

Hardy was in his early teens when Aunt Cora passed. He had not seen her in years. Being older, not necessarily wiser, did have its perks. His daddy needed him to help in various chores giving him an out when his mama paid her a visit. Rumor had it she had slipped on cat poop on the front porch and hit her head, dead when found by a mail carrier. Hardy's friends made light of her passing asking 'did you hear about the *catastrophe*? Cora the cat lady ran out of lives and rumor has it they buried her in cat litter.' He hated all the egging he was getting from his so-called friends, but he did not hold it against them. Aunt Cora was the butt of many jabs. Blood kin just made it worse. He never heard what happened to all those cats but a new Asian joint opened around the same time, a stone's throw away from Aunt Cora's house. It was the first time Hardy had heard the reference and correlation. His friends swore it was fact. They even made up menu items like Cora's cat chili, tabby tacos, kitty corn, Tom tatter tots, meow mush and feline fondue. It was all funny even if they were degrading his kinfolk.

Was it a wonder that the adult version of Hardy had almost lived a reclusive existence? Secluded and off the grid suited his disposition. A small circle of friends was welcome, friends more like family than what little family remained. Some might say he had outlived his close kin. Hardy would frame it differently saying he had out survived the like of them. Picking Steele to be overseer of his funeral arrangements had been a no-brainer. Steele would abide by his wishes spreading his ashes inside shotgun shells, no questions asked. Knowing Steele, he would get a kick out of doing it. Others would get their chance too if the shells and ashes lasted. It would be a mighty fine ending that would rival family quirkiness. If you can't ignore kin, just load up a bit of craziness to rival theirs. If Uncle Tom would have outlived him, he might have used his ashes for tattoos. Sisters *Prunes* came to mind.

50

Oh It's Frying Time Again, You Gonna Feed Me

Steele improvised the song that Ray Charles made famous singing "Oh it's frying time again, you gonna feed me…Hardy Bovine." Laughing, he thumped his fingers on the steering wheel to the tune playing in his head. There was nothing like a Saturday fish fry among friends. Fact, fish fries were good anytime. It was a mite early though, Hardy's invite for ten in the morning. He figured his friend must have a little socializing in mind first. It didn't much matter. He had Saturday off so why not spend it with his friends. For the occasion Steele had whipped up one of his specialties, the perfect 'fixin' for fried fish. It would be his surprise dish. Hardy had told him not to bring anything, but he figured he would appreciate the greens. Easing to a stop at Hardy's place it looked like he was the first to arrive.

Hardy was standing on the porch and offered a welcome wave. Steele exited his truck carrying the Dutch oven filled with his surprise. He offered Hardy a sneak peek inside the cast iron container. Hardy nodded his approval and told him to place it on the stove.

"There's a pitcher of sweet tea in the fridge if you want a glass."

"I'm good right now, maybe later."

"See you got the pickup running again. Did you ever find out who did it?"

"Ashamed to say I did."

"What's shameful about knowing?"

"Nothing, but my technique wasn't the most honorable method for flushing them out."

"Got me, let's hear it."

51

Steele recapped the episode eyeing Hardy for a reaction.

"Mighty bold tactics, Steele. It seems a bit out of character for you to take things to such extremes."

"Yeah, and it has bothered me ever since. Saving grace is that Red McClain was in on it and gave me the nod to carry it out. He invited me to supper last night. Get this. He made me the new foreman of the machine shop. Come Monday I go from one of the guys to their boss. It is not going to set well with some of them. To be honest, I am not sure how I am going transition into the position."

"It sounds to me that Red got rid of the worst troublemakers. I am betting the ones left will fall in line or the door will hit them on their backsides too. Don't fret it Steele, you will do just fine. Congratulations on the promotion."

"Changing the subject, isn't it a little too early to be having a fish fry?"

Hardy just smiled and offered no explanation or excuses. "It sounds like we have company."

"Yep, that's Sookie's Harley all right."

She rode into sight and Hardy remarked, "Sidecar."

"Two for so it seems," added Steele.

Sookie pulled to a stop removed her helmet and dismounted the bike. Eddy climbed out of the sidecar and took off his helmet too. She was glad he had taken her up on the offer. Here she would not be Sookie. She would be Susan.

"I figured we were both heading this way, so I offered Lover Boy a ride. Besides, I have not ridden this baby lately. She needs to know she is loved and appreciated too. How are they hanging boys?"

"There is cold beer in the fridge if you are ready to wet your whistle and sweet tea and soda for you Eddy."

"It's a little early for me and it is a little early for a fish fry too, isn't it?"

"Susan, now you, are y'all into time management all of a sudden?"

"Just early is all I'm saying."

"What about you Eddy, too early for you," asked Hardy.

"Shoot no, never too early for anything. I like pizza for breakfast."

"Well, we are not having pizza or fish for breakfast," replied Hardy.

Steele spoke up, "Hook, line and sinker then, I will bite, no pun intended, why so early?"

"I got no fish that's why."

"You did say fish fry, didn't you?"

"You heard it right. I did say fish fry, Susan."

"A fish fry with no fish sounds like it isn't a fish fry to me," said Eddy.

"I got rods and reels, cane poles, minnows, worms and crickets over yonder. Best we get to fishing and hope they are biting if we are going to do any frying later."

"Is this a joke, Hardy? I have never fished in my life."

"Gal, I reckon you better be learning then. Nobody here is going to be baiting the hook for you."

"Mister Hardy, I reckon I am a bit rusty too. I haven't fished since I was a kid."

"Lover Boy, in case you haven't noticed, you are still a kid. What about you, Steele? Do you fish?"

"Yeah, I can fish. I can seine, run trot lines, bottle fish, set baskets, spear fish and operate about anything that floats on water. But like Hardy just said I don't bait anybody's hook either."

"Susan, I reckon it is time we work through the learning curve and refresh the memory, Eddy," acknowledged Hardy. "What do y'all fancy, cane pole or rod and reel?"

"You're not joking, are you?"

"Susan, I never yank chains when it comes to fishing and frying," replied Hardy. "Besides, fishing isn't all about the fishing when you are among friends. There is no better way to partake of fellowship than among those that you cherish the most."

"So, it isn't about the fishing then," replied Susan.

"Well, if we don't catch any fish, we don't have supper. It doesn't mean we can't enjoy each others company and chew the fat. The way I look at it, we all know one another but we really don't know one another. Reckon this is partly because we each cherish our privacy and partly because we never bothered to ask."

"Why all the sudden interest in us, Hardy?"

"I don't know Steele. Maybe I'm a little melancholy."

"Not hardly…you are not the gloomy, saddened or depressed type. There is something else to this. What gives Hardy?"

"Cut me some slack, Steele. I'm old. Maybe I am a bit nostalgic to boot. There is no crime in learning about your friends, likes and dislikes, the fiber of their beings, what has made them who they are."

"Hardy Bovine you are not exactly an open book. You are as private as a person gets. Does this little fellowship experiment go both ways? Do we get to know the real Hardy Bovine?"

"I reckon that's how it is supposed to work if we do this right."

"What if we don't wish to open the chapters in our book," added Susan.

"Susan, I am not asking that any of you share what is not comfortable. I am just saying why not give it a shot. We do agree we are friends, right? Unlikely as ours seems, you got to admit it is unique."

"How so," asked Steele.

"Take me for instance. I am an old codger, and you are what, forty or so years younger than me. I am not one to judge a woman's age, but I am guessing Susan is at least a decade or more younger than you. And then we have Eddy, a mere teenager rounding out this motley crew. Quite a generation gap we have assembled and yet we enjoy one another's company and respect each other. There is something special about this connection we have. I just think it is worth exploring."

"Elderly wisdom?"

"Call it what you want, Steele. I like what we have. I just want to learn more about y'all. Is that so difficult to understand?"

"I hope this isn't an old man's last wish."

"What if it is, Steele?"

"You're not dying on us are you Hardy?"

"Not that I am aware of Susan, but I don't call that shot. None of us do."

"You are getting a little too mushy Hardy."

"There's nothing mushy about a little fishing and fellowship, Susan. What say you Eddy? You have been a might quiet."

"This fishing and fellowship stuff is sort of worrisome. I'm not good at either one of them."

"Maybe I overstepped my boundaries springing this on y'all out of the blue. I reckon I didn't think it was going to turn out to be so complicated."

"What the heck! It seems you have your mind set on doing this so I don't guess it would hurt any of us to give it a chance."

"Thank you, Steele, for humoring me. What about you two?"

"One stipulation," added Susan.

"Name it."

"If we don't feel comfortable with the subject matter we don't have to join in on the conversation."

"Deal! What about you Eddy?"

"I will fish if that is what everyone else wants to do."

"All right then. Choose you weapons over yonder. Ah heck, just bring everything and join me at the pontoon. We're going out on the river. Steele, grab that grocery sack over yonder. I made some cheese and bologna sandwiches in case any of you didn't eat any breakfast. I got a cooler on board iced with water, sodas and beer."

"Quite the host, aren't you Hardy," said Steele.

"Sandwiches and drinks are on me. The fish are on y'all."

"I can't swim," confessed Eddy.

"Got plenty of lifejackets on board but I would suggest you stay on board," replied Hardy. "Old Festus is an opportunist and you bobbing about out there might be a bit inviting."

"Old Festus, what's an Old Fetus?"

Hardy just winked and mustered a sly smile.

Trolling and Treading Water

The pontoon all loaded with fishing gear and those reluctant to use it, cast off with Hardy at the wheel. The river was broad but docile, perfect for leisurely wetting a few hooks. Eddy struggled to slip on and buckle his lifejacket all the while having visions of the S.S. Minnow and a three-hour tour gone badly wrong. If ever there was a Gilligan, he fit the persona to a tee while Hardy personified a crusty old version of the Skipper. Steele might pass for a much larger version of the Professor being that he was a machinist and good mechanically speaking. Jury was out on Sookie. She did not really fit the persona of either Mary Ann or Ginger. No Howells, they were short on millionaires, not that having any on board would increase their chances for catching any fish.

Susan 'Sookie' Cantrell was leery of the reasoning behind their host's suggestions. For as long as she had known Hardy Bovine, he had never been a man overly willing to share his personal business. Something stunk and it wasn't the fish bait. She was a private person and for good reason. Those reasons were her business, and no amount of fishing was going to make her share them if she didn't want to. Yes, these people were her friends, closer friends than she had ever had, but they were strangers as well to some extent. Hardy was right saying they knew one another but really didn't. Her life was far from being an open book. She preferred it this way. She wasn't ashamed of her past but on the flipside, there was no urgency to go there in front of her dear friends. She owed them nothing. They owed her nothing. She did her best to focus on the person she had become and not relive mistakes in her past. She had done her best to be happy and turn negatives into positives when possible. On this road called life she tried to take the good with the bad. She focused on smiling when she should be sad. It was easier to cherish what she had and not what she had lost. Forced forgetfulness trumped wallowing in past tragedies. Things will always go wrong; just remember the ride goes on. Life had often kicked her around, but she no longer perceived herself as a survivor, she had become a warrior. She had learned to be stronger than anything life threw at her.

Baiting a hook would pose no challenge but falling for the bait royally concerned her.

Steele eyed Hardy suspiciously. He cherished their friendship, but it had always been one with invisible yet respected boundaries. Something had changed this arrangement. Something had impacted Hardy Bovine's perception of their friendship. Whatever had, hadn't been experienced by the rest of them. He was forcing it on them in disguise of fishing and fellowship. It troubled Steele that this life changing event was troubling Hardy. There was nothing wrong with airing the dirty laundry if it was personal choice to do so. It bothered Steele that Hardy had somewhat made the decision for all of them. This disturbed him but he would never hurt the old man's feelings no matter what. What scared him was how he had lost his grasp on tactfulness recently. Bringing that gun inside the shop and threatening his coworkers with it had crossed a line even if he had the blessing from Red McClain to see it through. You never point a gun at anyone, even an unloaded one. He had done it though, no changing it.

Steele had broken a golden rule, justified or not, to expose the perpetrators that trashed his truck. No matter how educated, talented, rich or cool a person thinks he is, what is important is how a person treats other people that ultimately tell the integrity a person possesses. A person can fail plenty of times, but it is not a failure until the blame is laid on someone else. He took full responsibility for his actions as badly executed as they were. With Hardy he had kept the explanation simple; finding those who had done him wrong and making them pay. It had been partially true. Other more selfish motives had been involved. He was not prepared to expose the real Steele Dillon all for the sake of camaraderie and fellowship. Hardy had chosen this path, not him. We know each other but we really don't know each other had never been more powerful words. Did any of them really want to know the real person they thought they knew? Something told him that there were plenty of secrets to go around. Hardy sensed it too. Confessions do not necessarily set a person free. Fishing was the right term. Using the correct bait was a crapshoot. Hardy said choose your weapon, metaphorically speaking understood.

Hardy navigated the pontoon toward the perfect fishing spot wondering if he had done the right thing gathering them here. One day everyone will just be a memory. How a person is remembered is on the individual's shoulders. Why now you old fool, thought Hardy. Some days life is all about hopes and dreams. There is no perfect present or future. Other days life is a dang challenge, just putting one foot ahead of the other can be a victory. Either can be okay. The biggest mistake a person can make is constantly trying to prove their worth to the world. Focusing on it nets you nothing except forgetting your real value. Hardy always figured that living a satisfied life was better than living a successful one. Success was measured by others. What was important was the satisfaction measured in a person's soul, mind and heart. It didn't come down to what others thought. Sometimes good people make bad choices in life. Bad choices don't necessarily produce bad people. People are human, not any more complicated than that. The Lord didn't create perfect people. Flaws were abundant.

The challenge ahead as he saw it was how he was going to skin this cat; peal back the layers of the onion so to speak. What made him think it was his row to hoe doing so. Just because his eyes were now wide open did not mean the rest needed to be awoken to his revelations. He could lighten the mood and just fish for their supper and forget this nonsense. People deserved their privacy. He had surely cherished his. Some thought he was an off the grid recluse living way out here away from the rest of the world. In some ways that was exactly what he was. His job was his outlet, his connection to the outside world. He clung to it like a tick did to a hound. They didn't need an old fool like him at the prison, but he needed it. He had no social life without it.

Hardy sighed thinking, *Crazy old fart you have these wonderful friends and look at how you are apt to mess that up with your foolishness.*

Steele broke the silence, "Hardy, what's really up with you?"

"I figure trolling beats treading water."

"I thought we were going fishing," spoke up Eddy.

"Some fish fry," commented Susan. Nobody in this little circle of friends called her Sookie.

"One day you will wake up and time will be run out to do the things you always wanted to do. Reckon I have arrived at my time. I have always figured that I am best suited to be among the sounds of nature instead of the traffic and noise outside my little world has to offer. I was wrong with that notion. Sad it took me until now to open my eyes."

"You aren't dying on us are you Hardy," asked Steele.

"Hope not. I was raised. I didn't just grow up. My folks taught me to speak when I entered the room and say please, thank you and respect my elders. Reckon I resemble that notion now. I was taught not to be lazy and there has never been a lazy bone in my body, even now. Y'all keep in mind that you are supposed to give up your chair for people like me. That's what I have always practiced. Answer yes sir and no sir, yes ma'am and no ma'am. There is no replacement for respect. Hold the door open for folks and offer a hand where needed. Always treat people the way you want to be treated. All these are fine things that help mold a person, but a person has more to them that often meet the eye. To know a person, you must really know the person and to know the person that person must open up like maybe they never have. A big part of fishing is to know the proper way to troll. It beats threading water."

"You are dying aren't you," said Susan. "That's why we are here isn't it?"

"Dognabit, I am not dying. If I am, nobody has given me a death sentence. And before you ask, no, I have not seen my doctor lately. I don't even have a regular doctor. I am as healthy as a horse. Maybe healthy as an old mule but I am not sick or dying."

"Are we really going to fish then?"

"Yes, Eddy, we are really going to fish. A fry is not a fry without fish."

"I don't have a fishing license Mister Hardy."

"Don't fret it. Game management doesn't come out to this part of the river. This spur is off the usual boating route. Fishing is good. It isn't over fished. Matter of fact we are over a good spot right here. It's time to test your skills. Cane pole, rod and reel, red wigglers, minnows or crickets, pick yours and let's wet a few hooks, times wasting."

"What do you suggest I use?"

"Susan, you look like the rod and reel cricket type. Eddy, grab one of those poles with the red and white corks and bait your hook with a minnow."

"I am a rod and reel wiggler type," spoke up Steele, "and what about you, Hardy?"

"I am the captain, fish cleaner and fryer chef. Do me proud. Keep me busy boys and girl."

"Fishing and fellowship, huh," said Steele.

"Yep, y'all fish and I will supply the fellowship. Many folks fish all their lives never knowing that it isn't the fish they are after. Fishing isn't always an escape from life but often a deeper immersion into it. Most importantly, remember nothing makes a fish bigger than almost being caught."

"You are quite the fish philosopher aren't you Hardy," said Susan.

"Patrick McManus said it best, 'Scholars have long known that fishing eventually turns men into philosophers, but it is nearly impossible to purchase decent tackle on a philosopher's salary,' winked Hardy.

Steele assisted Eddy with the cane pole. The young lad was quite awkward handling the long pole, baiting it and then attempting to cast it. Steele offered a better technique, one saver for the rest on the pontoon, telling him to just lower it over the side. Within seconds the cork bobbed and then disappeared below the river's surface.

"Looks like you have snagged the first fish," said Hardy clapping his hands to certify his approval.

"Now what? How do I get this pole and the fish back on board this boat?"

"Steele, don't intervene. The boy must learn to do this himself," added Hardy.

Eddy continued his vicious struggle, the pole and the fish bettering everything he could toss at it. Susan paused preparing her rod to watch the battle of wits and brut force. Eddy was a far cry from being a brute to be reckoned with. So far, the fish was winning fins down. Eddy, red faced and frustrated looked about for help. Nobody offered any. It was him versus whatever was on the end of the line. He could barely hold the pole upright as the end of it bent to the weight and determination of the hooked fish. Exhausted, Eddy allowed the pole to rest on the pontoon's rail.

Hardy asked, "You aren't giving up are you, boy?"

Eddy shook his head no and again lifted the pole to no avail. There had to be a better way to win this tug of war.

Steeled whispered to Hardy, "Should have let him use a rod. That cane pole has him outmatched."

Hardy smiled and replied, "And he's got a fine keeper on the other end. The way that cork laid over on its side before it bobbed and went down, I'm guessing he has snagged a gar. His worries have only begun. Wait until he gets a look at the thing on the end of that line."

Susan overheard the covert conversation and joined in, "What the heck is a gar?"

"Predator fish, long and mean looking with a bill of a snout lined with razor sharp teeth," answered Hardy. "The minnow was easy eating for it."

"Glad my bait is a cricket then," replied Susan, her hook and line still dry and bait free.

Tiring again Eddy allowed the pole to rest on the rail a second time. An idea struck him. He began walking the pole hand over hand onto the boat. He found this method a piece of cake compared to holding the cane pole upright. He slid it until the tip end rested at the edge of the rail. He then grabbed the line with his right hand and then his left and began hoisting it up. Whatever he had caught was mighty heavy.

Hardy nudged Steele in the ribs and winked at Susan. The show had only begun. The young lad had a rude awakening in store if Hardy's hunch paid off. One thing for sure, it was young Eddy's fight to win or lose. Sad thing thought Steele that this was the first time the boy had ever fished. It was to be determined if it might be his last if this was indeed a gar. It wouldn't be long now; the cork having just broken the surface. Eddy fully engaged took a firm hold and gave it a mighty yank falling backward when he did. An elongated silver flash followed and landed in the pontoon. Hardy nor Steele had expected that last little maneuver. A thirty-five pound three and half foot long gar with a bill of razor-sharp teeth free reigned flopping about in the pontoon. Not known to be aggressive yet the toothy threat caused concerns among the craft's occupants.

Steele grabbed a paddle and swatted at it while Susan clambered atop a seat to protect her bare feet. Eddy took a cue from her and did the same while still holding the cane pole in a death grip. Not nearly as funny as Hardy had expected it to be, he quickly stepped on the fish and held it in place. He then removed the hook with a pair of pliers he retrieved from a nearby toolbox. Then he did something that shocked his passengers. He snapped off the bottom of the fish's elongated beak and then tossed the fish back in the river.

"That was a cruel thing to do," said a shocked Susan.

Eddy managed to ask, "What was that thing?"

"A gar is a predator fish, not good for much anything else as far as I am concerned. When they are around you can forget about the fishing spot. There are two ways to treat them once you have caught one. Do what I just did or use a stick and wedge their mouth open before throwing them back in."

"Both are cruel. Why not just kill it humanly?"

"There would be no fun in that. Besides, fishermen hate them."
"Why not eat them," added Eddy, now realizing his first catch had not been a keeper.

"They are editable but tough to skin, tougher to fillet. They don't taste like fish, more like alligator. It is an acquired taste that I have yet to acquire. Sorry Eddy, I know that was your first fish and it was a nice one, but there will be more before we are done today. Not this spot though. That gar has scared away the fish here. We will move on to another one of my prized honey holes."

"Nasty looking critter," added Steele, not insulted by Hardy and his actions.

All lines in, Hardy fired up the pontoon and headed to a new location. Eddy decided he no longer wanted to use the heavy clumsy to handle cane pole. He opted for one of rods and a change of bait too just in case another gar fish lurked in the new spot. Susan was not sure she wanted to fish after that despicable ordeal. Steele just took it in stride. Hardy was Hardy and never expect much more.

"We will be at our new spot shortly. Best everyone be ready to drop some hooks. It takes fish to have a fish fry. And it will take plenty of them to feed this motley crew of newbies to this wondrous past time.

Some consider fishing a sport. I refer to it as grocery shopping. The menu will depend on what we land. Hopefully that was the last gar."

"What if we don't catch any fish," asked Susan.

"We will catch fish. I have never been out on this river when I didn't; plenty of cats, brim, crappie and bass, all for the taking. Use the worms and bottom fish meaning do not use a cork. Just allow the sinker to take the baited hook to the bottom. When there is slack in your line you have found the bottom. Crank your reel until you remove the slack. For minnow and cricket fishing set your cork at about six feet from the hook. Toss it out there and you have a good chance of brim and crappie biting, maybe even a bass."

"You are just now telling us how to fish!"

"Susan, I first had to observe you and weigh your experience. That didn't take long, all except for Steele. Just take a deep breath and embrace what nature has provided us. Fellowship and fishing are tough to beat once you drop your guard and set free your apprehension. We will be at our next spot in ten minutes. Relax and enjoy the scenery."

Steele sat near the wheel and conversed with Hardy. "Was that really necessary, treating them like that?"

"How did you learn to fish, Steele?"

"No more surprises how about it?"

"You are a man of many secrets, aren't you?"

"You are not exactly an open book Hardy."

"It might be the day that we turn a few pages read some chapters. Like I said earlier we are friends, but we don't know much about one another."

"Does that mean you are going to join in on this little library book project?"

"I am a friend, aren't I?"

"Something is up, Hardy. What's troubling you and why is it important that we are involved in it?"

"There is a time for everyone to stop treading water, and instead sink or swim."

"You are not going to make this easy, are you, old man?"

"It has been said that there are three reasons why you shouldn't fight an old man. Number one: If you win you must face fact that you just beat up an old man. Number two: If you fail you just got beat by an old man. Number three: Most old men don't expect to lose in the first place and come packing with a gun. I'm that old man. I have been on the receiving end of a wooden spoon. I have been exposed to lead paint. I rode in vehicles that had no car seats and on bikes with a hard head, no need for a helmet. Riding in the back of a pickup truck was fun, not dangerous. I drank from a hose pipe and did not grow up on bottled water. I did not grow old from not taking risks or being taught the hard way. The four of us are from vastly different generations yet we have bonded. Why do you think that is, Steele? Don't answer. Just ponder and let it simmer a while."

"You are a tough read sometimes Hardy."

"Not really. I am a practical man. I give thanks for all that has happened in my life, the highs, the lows, the many blessings including the lessons. I have had my fair share of setbacks and spurts of growth. I am grateful for the jumbled life I have lived, not much more complicated than that. It is your choice if you decide to make it complicated. Sometimes it is easier to learn to trust the journey even when you don't understand where it is taking you."

"For a man usually of very few words, you have gotten quite chatty today."

"I read somewhere that life is not just about reaching a destination and fulfilling purpose, it is about discovering yourself as you travel on your journey to reach your destination. Old men don't become old men by ignoring the obvious. There comes a time, an awakening, when you realize that time is growing short to do the things you have always wanted to do."

"Is this your awoken moment Hardy, fishing and fellowship with friends?"

"Might be Steele, the treading or sinking to rock bottom, it is time to swim or drown."

"I would not say that too loudly. It's not a good omen when we are on the water."

"A pontoon is virtually unsinkable. A person's soul is problematic."

"Are we talking about friendship or soul searching, Hardy?"

"I reckon we are," he smiled.

Antagonizing a Protagonist

Hardy brought the pontoon to a stop and this time dropped anchor because the current was a bit swifter. He gave the command to wet the hooks. He even joined in this time to illustrate camaraderie in the outing. He no longer proclaimed to be the captain and mere nonparticipant. It was all for one, one for all. Plus, if they were going to have a decent fish fry, they must have a decent catch. The more hooks in the water improved their chances.

This spot was paying off quickly. Steele had hauled in two crappie and one brim. Hardy had focused on bottom fishing and had caught two catfish, both keepers. Susan had caught a nice brim as well. Eddy was the only one coming up empty so far. He had a few nibbles, but the nibbler had managed to strip the bait from his hook. Hardy observed him baiting his hook and identified the problem. He was only sticking the worm once. Hardy showed him how to loop the worm and impale it numerous times. After tweaking the technique, he caught his first brim. Not a big one but at least it had no ominous teeth. It was a bit small to keep but Hardy did not have the heart to tell him to toss it back.

"Steele, I have never heard you say where you originated before arriving here."

"You have never asked Hardy."

"I am asking now."

"Why now? Of what importance is it to you?"

"Why do you think it strange for a friend being interested in another friend's life? I'm old. Humor me."

"Fine, I was born and raised in Mississippi. Delta life, makes it feel homey being out on this river."

"Is that what brought you to the South Carolina Low Country, similarities maybe?"

"Purely coincidental."

"What then? You must have had a reason to migrate in this direction. I have never heard you mention having family in these parts."

"Don't have any, that's why."

"I feel like a dentist extracting deep rooted wisdom teeth. Your past seems a bit too painful to discuss."

"Why not leave the past where it belongs, in the past. Is it not better to live in the present and not dwell on yesterday?"
"Depends, I reckon. Was your past that bad? I say as long as you have memories, yesterday remains. Tomorrow hope awaits us but dealing with what bothers us can cleanse our souls."

"What makes you think something is bothering me?"

"Yeah, why are you taking such a sudden interest in his life, our lives? And don't tell me it is all to do with fishing and fellowship. Something else is eating you Hardy Bovine."

"Susan…Susan…should there be secrets among close friends?"

"Secrets are meant to be secrets and are personal to those keeping them. Secrets are not always meant to be shared even among friends."

"It's okay Susan. No harm no foul. Let him have his day of so-called fishing and fellowship and get it out of his system," added Steele. "Look Hardy, sometimes it is best for us to just accept that our past is over. Revisiting it, analyzing it, regretting it, sweating over it is not productive. It's over, done with and we cannot change it no matter how many times we dig it back up."

"See, you said it yourself. There is something in your past that haunts you. Sometimes it helps to talk about it. Once you do you can bury it for good or at least come to terms with it."

"Hey gang, look what I just caught," interrupted Eddy. "I think it is one of those crappie fish, a big one too."

"Nice one Eddy," said Steele. "Keep catching them like that and we will have all we need for the fish fry."

Eddy grinned from ear to ear, baited his hook and cast his line again. "By the way, I agree with Susan and Steele. Why talk about stuff we don't want to talk about. Let's just fish."

"See, even the kid gets it, Hardy," added Steele.

"Another reason I cherish y'all's friendships, honest as the day is long and no matter how I press, y'all are sticklers. I respect that but when I get an idea in my head, I am worse than a mangy old homeless hound that just latched onto a hambone. Call me the antagonist to a bunch of proud protagonists. Chapter one in the book of life, set the plot and forward the narrative. Allow me to back peddle a tad and try something a bit less intrusive."

"Being vague and evasive isn't exactly your style, Hardy."

"Just bear with me Steele. Any how, this little exercise involves all y'all."

"Fine, I need a fishing break," said Susan.

"Not me. They are biting my bait, but I will do whatever you want me to do Mister Hardy."

"I am going to toss out a few questions at you. All you got to do is answer yes or no, raise your hand or whatever when I pose my scenarios. How many of y'all have ever gone to a drive-in movie?"

Susan said no. Eddy asked what a drive-in movie was. Hardy provided an explanation, confounding the young lad even more. Steele remembered going as a child.

"Who has ever smoked candy cigarettes?"

"Smoked candy cigarettes how is that possible," asked Eddy.

"It is pretending not actually smoking."

Steele was the only one to raise his hand.

"Have any of you played a game of red rover, may I or Simon says."

Only Steele remembered some of these games.

"How about drinking from a hose pipe? Garden hose to some of you."

Everyone had.

"Times have surely changed but have any of you said the pledge of allegiance in a school class? We did this in the scouts too."

Sadly, none had.

"Based on the answers so far I should skip this one. Bet nobody ever watched American Bandstand or probably even heard of it. Figured as much. What about this, have you had a blood brother or sister? I can tell by the deer in the headlights looks that I lost you. It requires that you and your friend cut a finger and smear the blood between your fingertips…bonded by blood forever."

"Why in the world would any kid do that?"

"Never mind Susan.

A series of more scenarios were lost in translation: paint by numbers, collected S&H green stamps, drank Tang, shopped in a Five and

Dime, played tether ball. Hardy did receive a few positive responses to riding in the back of a pickup, eating veggies straight from the garden, clipped playing cards to a bicycle. He ended it by asking if anyone had used a rotary phone, listened to an 8-track tape or made Jiffy Pop popcorn. None of them had.

Steele posed the question, "Now what, did we pass, fail or require therapy?"

"I'll bite," added Susan. "What was the point of this exercise?"

"Hopefully to get to know one another better," replied Hardy.

"By asking us about things that probably happened in your generation," said Steele.

"Thought it might help but reckon I was all wrong with the easy approach."

"Easier said than done old friend," replied Steele.

"Excuse me Mister Hardy but it sounded to me like you were in a time warp or an escapee through a worm hole."

"Good analogy Eddy but I think it was more like H.G. Wells Time Machine falling down a rabbit hole," chuckled Steele.

"I wish I had lived back in a time before cell phones were around catching our wild and crazy moments for the world to see," sighed Susan.

"Okay Hardy, you have had your fun. Now what," asked Steele.

"Then I will cut to the chase, no more games and start by telling y'all something that you didn't know about me. I was an Army ranger in WWII."

"I don't know about Susan or Eddy, but I already knew you served in the military."

"Yes, you do but like most people who serve we don't like talking about it. Tell me something beyond you knowing I was in the Army, Steele."

"You know as well as I do that you have never told me anything about your time in the Army except that you are obviously a veteran."

"I learned something new. I didn't know," said Susan. "I guess I know where I fall in the friend rankings."

"Tied with me," said Eddy as he frantically reeled in another catch but had tuned in on the conversation.

"I was a kid, no older than Eddy when I enlisted. I found that I was a perfect fit for military life. I latched onto every aspect of it commencing with basic training. My superiors saw something in me as well. I breezed through every aspect of basics. My sergeant insisted that I should become a ranger, so I landed in Fort Benning, Georgia. There you learned quickly the rigors of fast walking in your boots with fifty pounds on your back. We did this every day plus we ran at least five miles three or four times a week while in full equipment. While wearing full uniform we also swam two or three times weekly. We completed airborne training and learned tactical training as well. More didn't make it than did. I became an elite soldier within one of the most prestigious military units."

"Hardy, we appreciate you sharing this with us, but we could have found this out through research on the internet or in the library."

"There is so much I cannot and would not share with you because the missions required the utmost security. I can tell you that one of my first missions was D-Day. My Ranger Assault Group attacked and captured La Pointe du Hoc the 110-foot cliff overlooking the English Channel occupied by the Germans. We lost over seventy soldiers and more than one hundred fifty were wounded. You can research this as well, Steele, but I was there slap dab in the middle of the horrific bloody battle. It was the first of many ranger operations.

I was a teenager, but I was a man among men. I found out that the young and the old bleed alike and dying does not discriminate by age. Death is tough no matter if it is friend or foe. I have never shaken the images from my mind. I remained in the rangers making my twenty years for full retirement. Leaving was the toughest thing I ever did. Serving ranked as the best decision I ever made."

"Thank you for your remarkable service, Hardy," said Susan.

"I was not sharing this to seek your thanks. I just wanted to illustrate that none of us are who we are thought to be. I was a tough son of a gun before I enlisted but afterwards, I was a spitfire full of piss and vinegar, hell bent on killing Nazis at any risks. Defending this great nation was my primary focus. I bled red, white and blue from day one."

"How many Nazis did you kill Mister Hardy?"

"More than any person should ever do. While the military does keep body counts, my focus was to complete the mission successfully and with as few casualties as possible. One loss was too many."

"Were you ever wounded?"

"Never Eddy, and I am not bragging about it. I lost people on either side of me, front and behind. Why the Lord saw fit for me to survive is his choice. It is not mine to question why them and why not me. Learn this, live it because if you second guess it, you lose your edge. Lose that edge and you skew your chances. I would like to say I controlled my destiny by being the best but that would be a lie. God called the shots. War is ugly and it has always been so. Many wars have been fought in the name of Christianity. Many have been fought for reasons defying logic. The consistent fact, men, women and children die when forces collide. A bullet or bomb cannot discriminate evil from good. Casualties are an almost certain outcome. I witnessed the worst of the worst and the best of the best."

"And do you carry any scars from your time spent," asked Susan.

75

"I look at it like this my dear. When something bad happens, you have three choices for dealing with the consequences. You can let it define you. You can let it destroy you or you can let it strengthen you."

"And which did you choose," asked Steele.

"All of them. You must work through the first two to arrive at the last. I don't think life is about the bruises and cuts you got along the way, it's more about the scars you accumulated to prove you at least showed up for the fight."

"Do you suffer from PTSD, Hardy?"

"What is PTSD, Steele?"

"Even I know the answer to this one Eddy. The acronym stands for post traumatic stress disorder. Lots of soldiers return from war adversely impacted by the horrors they were exposed to," clarified Susan.

"Like I said, anyone who served return with scars. They could be physical, mental or emotional."

"Which one is yours Mister Hardy?"

"The rigors of war always leave its mark. Enough said on that subject for now."

"Well played Hardy, now what?"

"Simple, Steele would you like to share one of yours? I am confident you had your defining moment like most of us have. The question, did you have one that broke you or made you?"

"You don't mince word do you Hardy?"

"Direct and to the point, a straight shooter mostly…"

"That you are but you have never been an open book. I'm just trying to figure out why now."

"Are you two gentlemen finished with this nonsense," asked Susan.

"That depends on Steele. Tell me Steele are you ready to share a few confessions with your friends?"

"I am not catholic. I am not required to confess my sins."

Susan took the bait. "Does that mean you have a sinful past, Steele? Nowhere works better than to share them with your friends, right? We are all ears and have broad understanding shoulders."

"See, she is on board," said Hardy.

"Then let her speak first," replied Steele. "Tell us Susan, where do your demons reside?"

Raising a Ruckus

Susan had been taken aback by Steele turning the situation on her. She was the furthest thing from an open book. Hardy was taking this getting to know your friends better a bit too far for her liking. Stubborn though, she did not appreciate anyone challenging her. Susan backed down for no one, not even friends. She thought about something she had read and filed away in her head, 'A bird sits on a tree never fretting that the branch will break but instead trusting on its wings.' Was this her time to take a deep breath and let it go? Should she focus on what was important and have faith that whatever she decided to share would somehow work out for the best, her best? How far was she willing to take this open friendship silliness? Fact was, nobody had ever asked her to share her past before. Nobody had ever been that close to her until now. Was this her moment? Could she relive what she had tried so hard to forget? Sometimes it was necessary to make a decision that might hurt your heart but heal your soul.

"Caught another huge catfish," yelled Eddy. "Hope everybody is getting hungry."

Susan took a deep breath then said, "I have always considered myself a strong person. Sometimes though, I need somebody to hug me and tell me that everything is going to be all right. I have not had one of those hugs in a very long time."

With that Hardy made his way over to her and pulled her close to him and whispered, "It is easy for any of us to underestimate the power of touch. It can be difficult for some of us to offer a friendly smile, a kind word, a listening ear, an encouraging comment. Any of these gestures can turn a life around if only we have the courage to act on them. The simplest act of caring can be a powerful tool for those needing the care. I am probably the guiltiest of all for not taking the time to act on any of these notions. For that I am sorry."

It was but a whisper, a man attempting to be honest about feelings he rarely ever shared, but the whisper was heard loud and clear by every one of the pontoon's occupants. Steele had never witnessed such sincere kindness by Hardy Bovine before. The man was practicing what he was preaching, opening up and showing his friends a side of him that they had never seen. While he cherished what was happening, he still questioned why Hardy had chosen this day to peel back his personal layers. Something had triggered it. Steele had a sinking feeling that the old man was keeping something from them, and he dreaded knowing the answer.

Susan broke the embrace and stepped back as if she had been stricken by a surge of electricity. She eyed Steele, Eddy and then Hardy as if either begging them not to pry or asking their permission to expose her soul. She was a tough one to read, always guarded, always Sookie personified. Beneath the leather and Harley persona there was a story to be told. Question, was she willing to tell it? She wiped back a single tear before sitting and then speaking.

"My mother and I moved here when I was fourteen. Before relocating here, we lived in Chicago. I never knew my father. My mother never talked about him and would never tell me anything about him when I asked. I still don't know who he is and whether he is dead or alive. Guess I never will since my mother is dead. She died when I was sixteen. I managed to make it on my own after she passed. I credit Frank 'Crawdaddy' Crawford with saving my life, giving me purpose and an opportunity. God rest his soul.

In Chicago we lived in the slums of Fuller Park, the south side five miles from the Loop. Saying we were poor and lucky to be alive was an understatement. Gangs ruled, still rule much of the city. To survive you learn to go along or look the other way. Some might say then move. Moving required money, funds we did not have according to my mother. My brother Terence was four years older than me, sixteen and in his prime. I was just twelve. My big brother was my best friend and protector from the evil that infested the area. Preteen and teenage young men were sought out in the criminal community. Gang warfare ruled. Murders and shootings were commonplace. We lived on the edge of chaos every single day. Various gangs had attempted to recruit Terence. He had successfully fended off most of them, but they were becoming more persistent. I witnessed several scary altercations between him and them. It was not uncommon for him to return home bloodied and bruised from their persuasive tactics.

I was twelve. Terence was walking me to school one morning when three thugs blocked the sidewalk ahead. Terence grabbed me by the arm, and we began crossing the street. They crossed the street keeping in stride and ahead of us. It was no secret that they were not going to allow us to pass. My brother eased me behind him as the three approached. None of them looked any older than him. They said nothing, just muscled him from my grip and escorted him up the street and out of sight around the next block. I walked to school and then returned afterward alone. I told my mother what had happened thinking she would call the police. She didn't. My brother did not come home that night or any night there after."

Eddy had paused baiting his hook, "What happened to Terence then?"

"Mother told me he was dead. She wouldn't tell me how she knew that he was. I saw those same three boys only one other time about a month later. They had been shot two blocks from where we lived, all dead. My mother and I were returning from the market. The spot where they died had been marked off with that yellow police tape. I told mother that they were the ones that had taken Terence. She shushed me like she did not want the police to hear me. I did not understand why. I should have asked but I didn't.

Maybe three months later police showed up at our front door and talked to my mother. She told me she had to go with them but didn't say why. Later that night she returned home alone. She had been crying. She would not tell me anything about what had happened."

"What do you think happened?"

"I think they found my brother, Hardy."

"Was there no funeral," asked Steele.

80

"No. Mother didn't mention anything about it then. I am just speculating now. I think the police might have asked her to come with them and identify his body."

Eddy asked, "Is he dead or not then?"

"I believe it was him and she refused to say it was him. I am not sure how she pulled it off, but we moved out of Chicago when I was fourteen. We lived with relatives for a while in Atlanta, Georgia before moving here. Mother was never the same though. I was sixteen, the same age as Terrance when she overdosed and died. She left an envelope addressed to me. In it she confessed that it had been Terence in the morgue identified as a John Doe. He had been shot four times. She told the police that it was not her son. In the letter she explained she had done it because she did not want her son to be associated with drug dealings and that she did not have the money to bury him. She instead allowed him to be buried by the city in an unmarked grave. She had struggled with this decision and eventually could take it no more and took her own life. I hated her for what she had done. At that moment I considered taking my life. By the grace of God, I came to my senses, but it sent me down a dark path as well. Something in me would not allow me to venture down the drug path. Lucky for me Cousin Howie Buzhardt and his wife Naomi took me in and offered some stability into my troubled life. Not until Cousin Howie introduced me to Crawdaddy and the Harley shop did I find my calling. Until now I have never shared this, not even with Crawdaddy who I loved dearly."

"Nobody ever expected you save the world gal, or you would have been born wearing a cape and tights. Best you can do is keep your chin up and survive as best you can," said Hardy.

"Wiley Fritz soothed my bruised ego telling me that having a bad attitude was like having a flat tire. You can't go anywhere until you change it. I sarcastically came back at him saying that I didn't have a bad attitude; I just had personality that he couldn't handle. Wiley was the second-best thing that ever happened to me taking me under his wing at the shop."

"You honored Wiley by naming that motorcycle club after him," said Steele.

"I wish I had a Harley," said Eddy now wetting hook again.

"All right Hardy, are you satisfied now? You got one of us to open up on this special friends and fellowship fishing expedition?"

"It's a good start Steele to a long day ahead."

"If Eddy keeps hauling them in, we should have plenty for the fry."

Hardy peered inside the cooler and said, "Not nearly enough yet to feed the appetites of this bunch."

"Maybe you should have kept the gar," ribbed Susan.

"Do you feel better now that you have come clean with the agony that has haunted you," asked Hardy.

"Maybe I suppose. With everything that has happened, I guess I can live my life sorry feeling for myself or treat what happened as a gift in a strange way. I have mostly treated it as a terrible obstacle to overcome but now I see it as an opportunity for me to grow from it. Moving forward hopefully I can learn to love the sound of my feet walking away from the tragedies that were not meant for me if that makes any sense at all."

"If it makes sense to you, is all that counts," replied Hardy.

"I have a question for you," spoke up Eddy.

"Ask away," she told him.

"Why don't any of us call you Sookie like they do at your shop?"

"Only my real friends call me Susan. Those that know me as the badass Harley babe call me Sookie."

"I like Susan better than the badass version," said a smiling Eddy. "Hold on, I got another bite."

Not Your Daddy's 'Gunsmoke' Episode

Eddy reeled in another catfish. He had latched on to bottom fishing and was a one-man fishing dynamo. This honey hole had been paying off nicely. Eddy was hauling in four to everybody else's one. He grinned with every catch. The boy that had never fished before today had found his calling.

"What tastes better, catfish, brim or crappie," asked Eddy.

"Which ever one is being battered and fried," answered Hardy.

"I am partial to catfish," added Steele. "Especially those fried crispy tails."

"I am betting that anything you catch will be the best you have ever tasted," said Susan.

Suddenly the pontoon tilled forward catching everyone by surprise. Susan almost fell overboard. Eddy did fall on his duff the hooked catfish flopping about on the pontoon floor. Steele was seated sensing that something had gone wrong knowing they could not have hit anything because they were anchored. Hardy eyed the bow and immediately identified the problem.

"Careful folks, we have company," he said motioning to the platform on the pontoon's bow.

Eddy still sitting on the floor could not see what he was pointing toward. Steele could make out something from where he sat in the back. Susan, after she had found her footing, had an unobstructed view of what had caused the pontoon to list forward.

"Don't anyone make any sudden moves. We have company," warned Hardy.

Eddy scrambled to stand and secure his fish ignoring Hardy's explicit instructions. Then he caught sight of what Hardy and Susan were staring at. "What the heck is that thing? It's humongous!"

"Old Festus, king of the river," whispered Hardy advising Eddy to lower his voice and minimize his movement because Eddy was standing closest to the bow.

"Is that a crocodile," whispered Susan.

"Alligator, all thirteen and half feet of it," answered Hardy. "I think Festus must have been attracted onboard by all the fish blood in the water."

"Are you saying it is my fault?"

"It is nobody's fault Eddy. Festus is huge and has an even bigger appetite."

"Well, he isn't getting my fish. I caught them. He didn't."

 Steele rose to where he could see the behemoth stretching across the bow. Festus was making a guttural growl followed by a hissing sound. The gator's mouth was hinged wide open. To say the sight of this prehistoric creature was scary was an underestimate.

"I agree with Chief Brody from that Jaws movie, we are going to need a bigger boat," said Steele.

"I'm not giving up my fish," repeated Eddy.

"I'm not getting eaten because you won't," demanded Susan.

"Stay calm folks. Don't rile Festus."

"Sounds to me like it is already riled with all that noise it is making."

"Territorial tactics Steele…"

"Since when does this pontoon belong to it," asked Susan.

"Since it decided to climb on board," answered Hardy.

"It's your boat and you seem to be on a first name basis with it, why not invite or insist that it leave."

"Maybe you would like to ask Festus to get out of town Mister Dillon," said Hardy to Steele without cracking the slightest smile.

Festus slapped its enormous tale against the pontoon, a thunderous sound in such close proximity. The gator was becoming more aggressive by the second now whipping its head back and forth. The pontoon tittered and bobbed forward with its every movement.

Frozen like a statue Eddy barely mustered a whisper, "We're all going to die."

"We should let it have this pontoon and the fish and swim for it. Shore is not that far away."

"Susan, I can't swim," whispered Eddy. "That's why I have been wearing this lifejacket."

"Trust me Eddy, you don't want to be bobbing about on the water wearing that," advised Steele.

"I'm not crazy. I'm not getting in the river."

"Nobody is going overboard," said Hardy in his regular toned voice. "What then Captain Hardy," asked Steele. "I don't think time is on our side."

"Eddy listen very carefully and do exactly what I say," instructed Hardy.

"Why me?"

"You're he closest," answered Hardy.

"I'll swap places with any of you," Eddy replied.

"One fish, the catfish on your line," explained Hardy. "Raise your rod as high as you can and try to dangle the fish in front of Festus. Lure the old boy into the water. With any luck he will take the bait."

"It's just one fish," added Susan.

"Do you realize what you are asking him to do," spoke up Steele.

"I am open to other suggestions Steele if you have any. And if you do, you better make it quick. Festus is growing impatient and probably unpredictable. If he comes over that rail, we are all screwed."

"I'm screwed first because I am the closest," whispered Eddy.

"Calm down Eddy and just do what I ask," repeated Hardy.

"You're asking a lot of that young man."

Hardy nodded as Festus shifted its weight appearing to position itself for a maneuver no one wanted to see it do. It had closed its massive jaws slightly eyes focused and daunting.

"Eddy, raise your rod slowly and then dangle that catfish just out of reach of Festus. On my say so release the line into the water. With any luck the old boy will go in after it."

"And if it doesn't," asked Eddy.

"We won't know if you don't try, son."

"This is no gar we are messing with," said Steele to Hardy.

"No, it isn't," replied Hardy. "Eddy slow and easy, we are depending on you."

Steele did not like this plan. Eddy had just learned to fish and now Hardy wanted him to take on this monster. It should be him or Hardy doing it, not the boy. One thing for sure, this standoff was getting them nowhere except closer to Festus making its inevitable move. Steele sighed thinking he could never live with himself if anything horrific happened to Eddy.

"Eddy, slow and easy, you can do it," instructed Hardy.

Steele reached for one of the cane poles. "Don't do it Steele," warned Hardy. "You will just piss the old boy off and provoke an attack."

"It's going to attack any way, why allow it to happen on its terms?"

"We can't win this fight, Steele. Our best chance is to lure it off the pontoon. Time is wasting. Eddy it is now or never."

Eddy had a death grip on the rod and reel, but he slowly lifted it. The movement instilled the hooked catfish to flip about. The noise of the floundering fish caught the gator's attention, and it moved slightly in that direction. Eddy noticed the movement and slowly but surely lifted the fish to stop the commotion. No denying it now, Festus was drawn to the fish. Question remained; would it stay put while Eddy finished what Hardy wanted him to do?

"Easy does it Eddy. Slowly, don't rush it. No sudden moves…"

Eddy now raised and guided the fish to where Hardy had instructed him to do. The catfish dangled just in front of the gator as he inched it toward the side. With lightning speed, the gator lunged and snapped up the fish, hook, line and sinker. Hardy started and gunned the pontoon in reverse. Festus flipped forward and off the platform into the water snatching the reel from Eddy's hands and the young lad falling to his knees.

"Pull up the anchor, Steele."

Steele hand over fist retrieved the anchor and they were quickly on their way. "You never expected the gator to dive overboard and take the bait, did you?"

"I reckon that was a remote possibility," answered Hardy. "Kind like you knew that pistol had no live ammunition loaded when you bluffed the boys at the machine shop. It's all in the bluff and element of surprise."

"Are we done fishing Mister Hardy?'

"Not yet, Eddy. We're just going to a safer spot. Plenty of time left yet."

"You've got to be kidding," commented Susan.

"He's not," answered Steele. "More fellowship in mind, huh Hardy?"

Hardy did not flinch nor respond.
"The gar ruined your first fishing spot and then this behemoth gator spoiled the second one. Strike three cannot be promising given your track record thus far. Don't you think it is time to cut our loses and settle for what has been caught?"

"Mister Hardy we were almost eaten back there."

"Eddy, Festus is not a man eater."

"Maybe your pal Festus isn't yet, but he came mighty close adding us to the menu," surmised Steele.

"That was my second close call with the grim reaper," added Eddy. "I'm not a cat. I don't have nine lives to squander."

"Second…," inquired Susan as she inched closer to the young lad.

Mighty Miracle Moment

Eddy still shaken by the gator's intrusive behavior unceremoniously flopped down on a cushioned seat. He wiped sweat from his forehead with his shirttail then glanced at the wake being caused by the pontoon's exit almost expecting to spot Festus in pursuit. There were no signs of the alligator but that didn't mean it wasn't there somewhere in striking distance. It did not grow that large and old from being stupid. Eddy, as uncomfortable as he felt tuned and said, "At least we saved our fish. Well, all but one…"

"How long are we going to stay out here," asked Susan.

"As long as it takes. The bad news is that time flies but the good news is that you must never forget is that you are still the pilot," replied Hardy.

"I believe in miracles because I am one," said Eddy as he stood to declare what only he presently knew. "My mom told me that there was only one reason that I am still here. It was because God decided it was not my time. He made a way for me. I don't know if that is true or not, but she believes it."

"And what miracle has the Lord worked to secure your place among us Eddy," asked Hardy.

"Eddy don't let the old coot pressure you into telling something private," said Steele. "No insult intended Hardy."

"None taken Steele. Young Eddy has the rite to say what he wants to say or not. I surely didn't mean to press our finest fisherman in any way."

"You men enjoy beating around the bush, don't you? You mean what you say even when you don't say what you mean. And you call yourselves straight shooters. You accuse us of gossiping but y'all flap your jaws as much if not more that women do. I've been listening but I am hearing more bull crap that talk worth listening to.

And you Hardy Bovine, what makes you the man in charge with all this neediness to know other people's business? I told you mine. Leave Eddy alone. This is no silly nonsense game. I learned a long time ago that it is foolish for me to ask God to change my situation when all along He wanted the situation to change me. The only keeper of my happiness is me with His help of course."

"That's a might winded for what we are used to hearing from you, gal," said Hardy.

"Pay no attention to him Susan. I heard you loud and clear, profoundly so," interrupted Steele. "It is never a good idea to allow others to have the power over you and what you think or say. Only you have that power to control the simplest things like a smile, your worth and your attitude. Bravo I say."

"Do you think we have really seen the last of that alligator?"
"Old Festus satisfied his curiosity Eddy. He won't be bothering us again today."

"All this talk Mister Hardy, is this what you had in mind by fellowship while fishing?"

Hardy smiled, "Only if it stirs your fancy son. Like Steele just said, the power and control belong to you. It doesn't matter what the rest of us think or decide."

"I have leukemia. They diagnosed me with it when I was just a kid, a real small kid. Did you know that there is no cure for it? Some say I am living on borrowed time. Right now, I am in what they call remission. Remission doesn't mean I am cured. It just means any signs and symptoms are less the factor for the time being. This is my third time being in remission. Third time is supposed to be the charm some say. My mom calls me a walking, living and breathing miracle baby."

"Dang it son, you have suddenly gotten as chatty as Susan," winked Hardy.

"Fellowship," whispered Steele.

Hardy heard him, "Fishing with friends can't be beat."

"I was barely two when my mom said she and Daddy knew something was badly wrong with me. They said that my stomach was always hurting, and I was hardly eating enough to keep a mouse alive. They took me to our family doctor, and he said it was just a phase I was going through, not to worry suggesting I would grow out of it. I didn't. Things only worsened. According to my parents I started having bouts of shortness of breath. A kid just wants to rip and romp, and I was not able to hang with my friends. Something was always hurting me, my muscles and my joints so they told me when I was old enough to understand. They ended up taking me to another doctor recommended by ours, a specialist. They said he identified that I had an anemia problem and to make matters worse I had an infection. That doctor sent me and my parents to another doctor, an oncologist. I was too young to understand any of this poking and prodding."

"It must have been tough being a child dealing with this," interrupted Susan.

"Luckily it is mostly a blur. I don't remember most of it other than what my parents have recapped for me. It was only the beginning of what was ahead for me, for them. My parents had started noticing tiny red spots on my skin, bruises and bleeding issues. These were leukemia signs too. The oncologist told them that most children have very high remission rates, some up to 90%, and that eventually they can go into permanent remission and lick it. Not me, I landed in the 10% rate. Beating it was not in my immediate future. Mine was the acute kind. I didn't know it back then but later I found out that my chance for licking it was not good. I have what they call CML, chronic myeloid leukemia. It affects my bone marrow. It usually shows up in old people, rarely in kids; lucky me. Thankfully I was too young to remember the trauma of chemotherapy and all that goes with it.

92

They chased it into remission. The next time it showed up I was almost eight. That one I remember. I did not fully understand everything that was happening, but I do remember. I spent a lot of time in and out of the hospital. I missed school and time with my friends. I couldn't be around family gatherings during that time because my immune system couldn't fight off normal stuff. It sucked. Finally, though it went back into hiding again and my life returned to as normal as it could be. My parents stressed out over it more than I did. I was a kid and had no idea I was so close to dying. Kids don't die or that's what I thought.

Last time I was sick was two years ago. It was the worst one. Maybe because I was old enough to understand everything, including the dying part. I am out of the woods for now, but my doctor doesn't think I am going to beat it. He didn't say it in so many words. Doctors don't like to set time limits but there is something about the way he acted and talked to me, and how my parents have acted since that last time that makes me think I don't know everything that I need to know. Mother just keeps calling me her miracle child. Daddy doesn't call me that. I don't think he buys into it like she does. As for me, I try not to think about it. Trying doesn't always work. Every time I get a bruise that doesn't heal quickly, or I have a breathing episode it sends me into a panic attack. I don't want to die, not yet. I am too young. There is so much stuff I have never done. Like fishing and surviving my first alligator attack."

"Sorry Eddy, we didn't know," said Steele.

"That's okay. It isn't something that I talk about. People look at me differently when they know. They treat me like I am easy to break. Some just push away. Others seem to think they can catch it or something. I want people to treat me like I am normal."

"You are normal Eddy. Take it from one that knows, you must learn to believe in yourself well beyond any limits you thought possible. Your life is worth a lot more than you believe it is. If you get your head straight you can do anything you want to do."

"Susan is right," added Steele. "Believe in yourself. You are our friend, a regular fishing dynamo at that. Don't worry. I think I speak for all of us when I say that your telling us will change nothing in the way we treat you."

So far Hardy had said nothing. This was more the Hardy that Steele was used to being around. Yes, he was always opinionated and never shied from sharing his opinions, but he rarely got involved in any deeply personal discussions. He always respected a person's privacy and kept his distance when it came to his. Steele eyed him trying to read into this alleged fellowship outing. Something more was involved. Hardy had an agenda, fishing them like a new honey hole and he did not appreciate the old man's tactics. Why now? Why was him knowing their business suddenly so important? Did he dare pose that question? For now, he straddled that fence.

"I just want to do stuff and be somebody."

"Think about it Eddy, you told me that you had learned to play chess in a blink and had then defeated a guy that was supposed to be good at it," Susan reminded him.

"Who was this fellow that taught you to play chess," asked Steele.

"Funny name, he was on the bus that had engine trouble that stopped by Pop's. I believe his name was Luigi. He didn't tell me his last name."

"Luigi...Luigi Caruana," asked Steele.

"I don't know, maybe. He just wanted to play and teach me how to play while waiting for the bus to get fixed. He even had his own chess set with him. He said it was from some place called the Staunton House and they were made from a zillion year-old wooly mammoth bones."

Steele was awe struck, "It had to be Luigi Caruana. If it was, the man you beat is a world-famous chess grandmaster, Eddy. That trumps fishing and escaping from alligators, hands down."

"I know he didn't seem happy that I beat him. I won in four moves. I didn't even know I could win in four moves until I realized I had him in checkmate. He seemed crazy surprised too."

"Does that make me a chess grandmaster?"

"It does in my book," said Hardy adding in his two cents worth.

"Do you play chess Mister Hardy?'

"Nope, I am a checker man like you but if I were you, I would focus on chess. Might be that you have found your calling."

"I have a checkerboard, but I don't know where I can find wooly mammoth pieces."

"Lower your expectations, lad. I bet we can find you a nice plastic set," said Steele.

"That would be super. Do any of you know how to play?"

"You can teach us," added Susan.

"I don't know. I have only played that one time and it was over before we really got started."

"Get ready to drop your hooks. We are almost at my favorite spot," advised Hardy.

"Hope it is gator free," smarted off Steele.

"On this river there is no such thing as gator free. Most gators are not like old Festus. They are as afraid of us as we are of them. Put that last little episode behind you and just focus on filling up that cooler," said Hardy with a smile and a wink.

Out of the Fire into the Skillet

There had been no more gator encounters. Hardy had been dead to rights saying old Fetus would not be a threat the remainder of their little fishing jaunt. They did see a couple of small gators, but they had given the pontoon wide berth. Eddy did not take his eyes off them until they swam out of sight or slipped below the surface. Susan, while not as concerned, did keep a wary eye on them as well. Steele's primary focus was still on Hardy Bovine. He was convinced more than ever that his friend had an ulterior motive for inviting them to this fish fry. While it was not uncommon for the four of them to occasionally gather at his place, this time was different. Riding on the pontoon was not out of the norm but they had never been designated as fisherman. Each of them had been invited to a fish fry. None of them had imagined that the fish fry would depend on how successful they would be at catching the fish. Steele held firm to his suspicions that them being here had nothing to do with frying fish; at least not any that were caught form the river. The old man had something else up his sleeve and had yet to play the winning hand.

Susan felt a bit liberated having opened up a bit on what had molded her life for bad and good reasons. She still struggled with the forgiveness part though. Her mother had no right doing what she had done concealing her brother's death like she had. Even worse, she had taken the cowardly way out by committing suicide. Only then had her mother exposed her dirty little secrets. Terence's life had never been celebrated. While she had grieved his disappearance, she had never had the chance to really grieve the loss, his death. Closure at her mother's hands had been no closure at all. Susan now faced life without her mother, her brother and a father. Why hadn't her mother had the courage to tell her instead of writing it on a piece of paper? Furthermore, why hadn't she allowed them to give Terence a proper burial? Dead was dead no matter how he lived his life or how he died. Her mother had been ashamed of the life he had chosen but what if it had not been his choice? She had been with her brother when he had been taken away by those other boys. He had either been forced to do their bidding or more likely had been murdered for refusing. Her mother had used the excuse of not being able to afford a proper funeral and burial. What a cop out! It's always better to tell what you know and how you feel because if you don't those opportunities are lost in a blink. Regret can last a lifetime. Her mother's regret had eaten her alive until she could no longer face what she had concealed. It had taken what Hardy Bovine had called fishing and fellowship to give her the strength to share the family's dirty little secret, out of the fire into the frying pan.

Hardy Bovine walked over to the huge cooler and peered inside. "Well folks it looks like we have ourselves a fish fry for sure now. Thanks to young Eddy we will be eating well. Not to slight any of the rest of you, me included, but he did land the most. Son, I think you are a natural when it comes to fishing. You are welcome on my pontoon anytime."

"Thank you, Mister Hardy. I never knew fishing was so much fun. My father never took me, probably a long list of things my parents never allowed me to do. I fibbed earlier saying I had not fished since I was a kid. They tend to treat me like I am fragile and breakable even when I am in remission."

"Don't hold it against them. Your folks love you Eddy. Sometimes living the life someone else has chosen for you can make life tough and even unfair. You are forced to stay in your comfort zone instead of experiencing what lies outside that safety net. Fishing was a baby step, but it was a step just the same. Respect them but convince them to trust you and respect your wishes as well. Do this tactfully. Life is too short."

"In my case it could be even shorter Mister Hardy. I am not ready to die."

"My apologizes, Eddy, it was not my intention to say it that way."

"No sweat Mister Hardy. I like you telling like it is and not tiptoeing around it like my parents do. I get it. Everybody is going to die sooner or later. I just hope mine will be a lot later than sooner."

Steele admired Hardy and his candidness. He never held back any punches even with Eddy. Eddy deserved as much too. The kid understood his predicament and was taking it like a man. Nobody wanted to die, especially to die young. Facing a life-threatening situation was not the best of circumstances. Steele understood the ramifications. Death sentences are not always disguised as incurable diseases. Nobody knew this better than Steele Dillon. He preferred leaving the past where it belonged. Unlike the others and their turns in the confession booth, he wasn't game on playing this out like the others had. No amount of fellowship and fishing had worked its magic on him. His way was to remain positive and avoid conflicts. Well, he had obviously done a bit of backsliding back at the shop when his truck had been violated. Being positive doesn't necessarily mean that you don't ever succumb to negativism. It just means that you don't allow the negative thoughts to control your life. That uncomfortable episode was in his taillights. It had been faced, addressed and settled to his satisfaction.

"Hey Steele, what's got you wandering off so?"

"What do you mean Hardy?"

"I can tell when a man is mind drifting. Face never lies. It is funny how a person's expression can tell a story even when it isn't an intended choice. You had that look, deep and profound. Where were you?"

"You try to read too much into everything. Next thing you'll want to do is tell our fortunes like Madam Alicia over on Carlyle Road. Do you have a crystal bowl stashed away some place?"

"Madam Alicia huh, been there very often or if you tell maybe, it ruins the predictions?"

"Hardy I am not sure what angle you are playing today but as sure as I live and breath you are up to something. I haven't put my finger on it yet but mark my words I will."

"Steele Dillon since when did you become so paranoid?"

"Paranoia has nothing to do with it and you know it. What are you really up to today, asking us here and then launching this hokey fishing trip?"

"Hokey my big ole butt, a fish fry requires fish. We set out to catch them and we did. I would say today has been successful on all counts."

"What if we hadn't caught enough fish for your so-called fish fry, then what?"

"Barking up the wrong tree old pal because we did, didn't we? I know this river like the back of my hand. Fish are plentiful if you know where to find them and I do. That being said I didn't expect old Festus to crash our party. You got to admit though, that was quite the hoot encountering the old boy, wasn't it?"

"I don't know about Eddy and Susan but I'm not buying it Hardy."

"Sometimes we know deep down what we really need to do, but we can be afraid to do it. Often it means taking chances and relying on your gut. Like young Eddy stepping out of his comfort zone, baiting and wetting hooks. Without risk there is no reward. It is how we grow, understand and appreciate life. It's not a complicated process Steele if you are willing to give it a shot."

"Like I said, you are playing us Hardy. I'm not sure why but you are. I for one do not appreciate your tactics or understand your motive. Honesty is supposed to be the best policy and never is it more important than among friends."

"Come now Steele Dillon, you are not calling me out as being dishonest, are you?"

"Boys, I think you need to cool this banter you got going on between you. I thought we were here as friends for fellowship and a fish fry. We have plenty of fish to fry without tossing one another into the skillet."

"Susan, I apologize for my part in this little discussion," said Hardy.

Steele nodded as well, "Me too," but then he whispered to Hardy, "I will figure this out. Count on it."

"All is forgotten and forgiven I do hope," added Hardy as he locked eyes with Steele offering him a little Hardy Bovine sarcastic wink. "Eddy, pull up that anchor. It is time you learned the art of cleaning what you caught. We have fish to fry."

"I am ready Mister Hardy."

"I will leave the excitement to you boys. I would not wish to steal your thunder and male bonding," added Susan.

"I forgot to add my dear that you always clean what you catch. As memory serves me you caught five of what is in that cooler. This is no different than a person shooting their first deer. Blooding the hunter is a given."

"What makes you think this is my first fish?"

"Chicago doesn't offer many opportunities for casting baited lines. If I am lying, I am dying, gal. Besides you confessed earlier that you had never fished. Watching you figure it out told me all I needed to know."

"All right, you got me. I guess this is part of your odd fellowship experience."

"Indeed, it is," winked Hardy.

"I will think twice before I accept another invitation to a fish fry, especially one from you Hardy Bovine. I never expected I would be baiting, wetting and cleaning my way for a meal. Is this the going rate for friends and fellowship?"

"Touché gal, the friendship and fellowship are free. Now the fish fry comes with a little catch."

"I get it Mister Hardy…catch…that's funny. Anchor is up."

Hardy navigated the pontoon back down the river. Eddy gobbled down the last cheese and baloney sandwich. Steele smiled watching him thinking about what the boy had endured in such a short lifetime. Susan eyed Steele wondering what he meant about what Hardy was up to. She dearly loved everyone but realized too that this little outing was out of the ordinary even for Hardy Bovine. She did not like secrets, not that she mistrusted any of her dear friends. Hardy was a sly old fox. She knew as well as Steele that he had never been an open book before so why now? Could it be that what Steele had suspected that Hardy was really dying? Hardy said he wasn't and that was not something you lied about, especially among friends. Her thoughts quickly returned to the premise of cleaning her five fish. Just how did you do it she wondered? Hardy had nailed her. She was born and raised in the inner city. What did she know about the wild kingdom?

It was mid afternoon by the time they returned to Hardy's place. With the fishing gear stowed away and the pontoon unloaded it was time for Susan and Eddy to learn the technique of preparing fish for frying. Steele was an old hand atit and could help with their training. Hardy had a fish cleaning table out back equipped with a sink and running water. Living off the river and the land one had to be prepared for what nature provided. While Hardy enjoyed pizza and other fast-food options, he loved to partake of Mother Nature's bounty even more. It was hard to beat fresh fish from the river and a rabbit or squirrel taken down as the main menu. If ever he had to, he could easily live off the land. The Lord had offered him a different path and means to provide for himself. Working at the prison had provided him all he needed to live a comfortable lifestyle.

"Time to learn the trade kiddies," said Hardy. "We got a variety pack, catfish, brim and crappie. All fish are not cleaned the same. Be thankful we didn't keep that gar, or this little lesson would require further consideration."

Clabber and Buttermilk took turns weaving through and rubbing against Hardy's legs. Hardy glanced down at the darn cats, nothing but a nuisance he thought. He would never admit just how fond he was of the two felines. No one at the prison knew that he had any pets, especially cats. He had a reputation to uphold. Hardy Bovine never got attached to any critter and few people. Those that knew him on the job saw a cold heartless loner, one to never be disrespected if you had any sense at all. He warned anyone attempting to wrongly cross him that he was old but added that he hadn't gotten old without some hard knocks along the way. He delivered a stern warning that he should never be judged by his old leathery cover. Test his wrath and be forewarned that doing so would be met with dire consequences. Nobody had ever challenged him. Hardy was far from the cock of the barnyard. He figured mostly he had been left alone because he was old and not because he was feared. There was no honor in beating up an old coot like him. Fact is it would probably ruin your reputation instead of emboldening it.

"Let's start with you Susan. You caught three brim and two crappie. Grab that scaler over yonder, gal."

"A what?"

"It's that little metal tool over there with the saw teeth. We are going remove the scales from these boogers first. Trust me when I say it, scales are not tasty."

"Here," said Susan offering Hardy the toothed thingamajig.

Hardy placed his hands behind his back. "The scaler is for you, not me. I got your fish lined up and waiting for you. Start with that fist brim."

Susan looked at him puzzled. "I thought you were going to show me first."

"There is no better way to learn than by doing it. Are you a righty or lefty?"

"I am right-handed."

"Then hold that fish firmly by its tail with your left and then using your right hold that scaler firmly and start scraping free the scales from its tail to its head. When you finish rinse it off under that spigot and then flip it over and do the same on the other side. Be careful around the fins and that spine back bone because they will cut you."

Susan caught on quickly and finished the first fish. Hardy told her to do the same for the other four. Then came the fun part, he explained, cutting off their heads and tail and then gutting their innards. She preferred removing the scales ten-fold.

"You did good gal. Nothing to it, right?"

"If you say so," she replied.

"Steele, why don't you get Eddy started with those brim and crappie he caught. We will save the cats for last."

Eddy had been watching Susan and not to be outdone had finished his perfectly. "What about the catfish Mister Hardy?"

"There is only one way to skin a cat," he winked. "Lose the scaler. You'll be using a knife and pliers. Grab that first nice one. Watch out for the fins you can get cut bad by them. Hold it by the head and then use that knife to make cuts behind its gills toward the head. When you finish cutting all the way what I explain you are going to peel it like a ripe banana. Don't cut off the tail like you did with the brim and crappie. We'll be saving the tail. It's the best part when we fry it. Folks fight over who gets the tails."

True to his word, Hardy and Steele cleaned the ones they landed. When all was said and done, they had a mess of fish totaling twenty-seven including some catfish that were filleted. No one would leave this fish fry hungry. Hardy intended to feed their faces and their souls. Plenty of fellowship remained before these friends would depart the premises. There were honey holes yet to be fished. It was up to Hardy to use the right bait to get it done.

"There's nothing like frying up fish in the great outdoors. Over yonder I got a gas operated eye and my seasoned iron skillet."

"That's the biggest skillet I have ever seen Mister Hardy."

"Steele, how are you at making hushpuppies?"

"If you got the fixings, I can hold my own but I have a better idea. Susan, would you like to learn the art of hushpuppying while Hardy teaches Eddy how to fry fish?"

"Why not, I have already done the hard part. How tough could it be to cook hushpuppies?"

"Got that deep fryer on the second burner Steele and everything else you need you can find inside, including lard. I prefer cooking with lard when it comes to frying."

"Lard, what's lard Mister Hardy?"

"Have you never heard of lard, son? It is rendered pork fat."

"My parents don't allow me to cook anything. It's that protective thing again."

"I already made cold slaw. It's in the fridge."

"I suppose if we hadn't caught any fish, we had slaw and hushpuppies on the menu," commented Steele.

"And what you fetched here in that Dutch oven," Hardy reminded him.

While everyone was busy with their assignments it was the perfect time for Hardy to do a little pondering. He watched his friends caught up in the moment and nodded. He thought about how you never really knew what impact you have on those around you are vice versa. He didn't do it nearly enough, but a smile can go along way too. The act of kindness worked its magic both ways. Kindness can make or break a situation, sometimes by entirely turning around someone's life. People of all walks of life can use a hug or someone willing to listen and engage in deep thoughtful talk. The problem though, it is not always easy for people to offer that first act of kindness, to lend a caring shoulder or ears to listen. Even among friends the difficultly and stubbornness can exist. Nobody knew this better than he. Righting wrongs, reconciling what ifs, overcoming pigheadedness doesn't always come easy. Pride and humble pie can be tougher than swallow than eating crow in the first place. Just what was he hopeful of achieving with this gathering? Was it selfishly for him or unintentionally for them or maybe all included?

"I'm too old for this foolishness and utter nonsense," whispered Hardy "Damn you Elrod Long for setting this thing in motion."

The whisper did not go unnoticed. Steele's ears homed in on every single word. He recognized Elrod Long as being the con that Hardy regularly played checkers with. The mystery yet to be solved was what Elrod Long had done to set this in motion. Whatever had gone down between them had profound consequences that had apparently rattled Hardy Bovine to the core. Hardy Bovine did not rattle easily if ever. Steele had latched onto his first break in this little orchestrated, far from innocent, social gathering. With the right bait he would snag him a Bovine. He must be tactful, not disrespectful, words chosen wisely, a trap laid discretely to uncover the mystery behind the man's madness. He hoped Hardy had not lied about dying. Hardy Bovine was not a liar. His word meant something when given. He might tiptoe around an issue if he was uncomfortable discussing it, but he would never lie to conceal it. He might even boldly say enough is enough, but he would not tell an untruth. Elrod Long seemed to be the key. Too bad he was incarcerated, or he might just go directly to the source. No time, this was playing out now and Hardy held the winning hand.

"Hey Steele, your feet are growing roots. The hushpuppies won't cook themselves and Susan isn't going to learn standing there over an empty deep-frying pot," shouted Hardy.

Steele gave Hardy a responsive salute to acknowledge he understood loud and clear. He then did what he often did. He mentally pressed his pause button. Thinking about what Hardy might be up to he paused before judging him. It was always good policy to pause before judging someone, even Hardy Bovine. For sure he needed to pause before accusing him of doing something he was reasonably sure he was doing. Pause before you react harshly. He had failed to pause before brandishing his gun at the shop when accusing those he was certain were guilty of the crime. The most important pause: avoid doing or saying something you will regret later. He was on the cusp of this one where Hardy was concerned. He did not appreciate what he seemed to be orchestrating at their expense. Pausing did not seem to be a feasible option. Friends do not mistreat friends. He snuffed out this thought immediately because there was no evidence that Hardy was mistreating anyone. He had been more than hospitable. That didn't change the fact that he was up to something, but up to what remained a haunting question.

Hardy had suspicions as well. Steele Dillon was acting and reacting strangely to conversations instigated by him. He wondered had he been overreaching with his prying ways. He had stated fact precisely at the beginning that he felt friends should know friends better if their friendships were genuine. He did not doubt that theirs was genuine but to really know someone you must really know them from their roots, what made them who they had become. Good and bad exited in people's lives. Nothing was as it seemed. Ugliness existed as sure as total happiness did. The question still existed though; what gave Hardy Bovine the right to know his friend's deepest and darkest secrets? He certainly couldn't rewrite their history to make everything all swell and wonderful.

His unorthodox technique seemed to be working. Both Susan and Eddy had cracked open the door a bit. Steele was the tougher nut to crack. His and Steele's relationship had blossomed for that very reason. Neither were willing to share much of their past. Up until now they had each respected that notion. Steele still did. It was he who had decided not knowing what was the best policy. Elrod Long was to blame for setting this in motion, for getting inside his head. A person's life is supposed to be defined by how they live their life and how they treat others. Hardy now had it in his head that there was more to it. As person comes to the end of life's road and it is up to every person to be decisive in how they wish to be remembered and how they prefer to be laid to rest. Before these factors can be settled though, he yearned to know more. To understand a person, you must walk in their shoes. Some folks were not keen on letting you wear their shoes. He should know. He had always been that way himself.

Old man's curse, too often the narrative and point of view changes when you find yourself on the backside of life. Perspectives can be skewed and influenced when one finds themselves walking down that last hill. No, he had never been one to fret over dying and still wasn't. Death did not scare him. Everybody died sooner or later. He lived by the mantra of being strong, not rude, being kind but not weak, being bold but not being a bully, being humble but not being timid and being proud without being arrogant. Mostly this worked.

With every objective, backsliding is always a possibility. Humans are not infallible. Hardy was the furthest from being a model citizen and perfect human being.
Cross him and he tossed a lot of what he should practice out the window. He was never one to start a fight or an argument, but he could damn well finish one with whatever means were necessary. Say what you mean and mean what you say. Don't back down. Back it up. He reckoned everything had flushed out because he was still standing and in reasonable health for a feller his age. Much of the younger generation give old people a pass when they say and do stuff usually not acceptable by younger folks. Pass or not he did not really care how people took him. He was not a babbling and drooling old fool yet so what they thought did not much count. Like him or not it was never his worry. Might be a bit of an exaggeration where friends were concerned. His small circle of friends was important and what they thought of him was just as important. Those friends were assembled for this fish fry. It was in his hands if he screwed up

those friendships with the nonsense that had overcome him. Not one to back peddle, his mind was set on its current path.

Hardy mouthed to himself as if to reinforce this fact, "I am who I am. I will never be what you think I should be. I will never be what you want me to be. I am me and always have been."

"Did you say something, Mister Hardy?"

"Yeah boy, I was just thinking out loud. Take what you learned today and never give up on who you strive to be. Take it in stride that today might have been hard, and tomorrow could be even worse but the day after tomorrow or some day hereafter will be nothing but sunshine."

"Whatever you say Mister Hardy; the lard has melted, what now?"

Hardy mustered a little smile and said, "Time to batter our fish. We will dip each fish in egg wash first then in a concoction of flower and corn meal seasoned with salt and pepper. It's not any more difficult that that. It's all in the timing and relies on Steele and Susan holding up their end cooking those hushpuppies. How's it coming Steele?"

"Susan is doing fine. If you are waiting on us, you are backing up."

"Don't let them rattle you Eddy. This isn't a competition. It's just better when the fish and fixings can be served up hot. Nix that. Cold slaw does not require any cooking," he winked.

"First fish is all coated and ready Mister Hardy."

"Hold it by the tail end and slowly ease it in the grease. Turn her loose before your fingers touch the hot stuff. That was perfectly done Eddy. You are as much a natural cleaning and cooking them as you are catching them."

"Thank you, Mister Hardy. That means a lot coming from you."

Hardy patted Eddy on the head and told him to add a few more and what to watch for to know when they were done. He glanced over at Steele and Susan, and they were progressing nicely as well. Hardy walked over to his outdoor wooden picnic table and spread a red and black checkered tablecloth on it and then set the table with sturdy paper plates. While paper plates seemed appropriate for the outdoors setting, he preferred real utensils to the plastic alternative. It was a fine day for a fish fry and fellowship with friends.

Corralling and Skinning Cats

During the meal there was considerable conversation, mostly light and jovial. The fish had been fried perfectly. Hardy introduced Eddy to the best part of catfish, the tails. He laughed telling the young lad how when his mama fried cats that the tails seldom survived making it the dinner table. This person and that were apt to pinch them off and eat them long before. There was something about crispiness of catfish tails. The hushpuppies were crispy and tasty as well but were no comparison. With perfect weather complimenting the gathering it had been quite successful so far.

"Steele, what you say we have a peek at what you brought in that Dutch oven?"

"Time seems to be about right Hardy. Everyone is finished with the main course. I'll fetch it; kept it warm in your oven."

Steele, gripping the Dutch oven with potholders, retrieved it and set it center table. The Dutch oven was Steele's all inclusive cooking preference. Just about anything could be cooked in one. Steele so enamored by the cast iron pot, had researched its origin. It had originated in the Netherlands in the 17th century thus accounting for its name 'Dutch.' They were constructed of a seasoned cast iron. If you had a one you could cook almost anything in it on the stove top, inside the oven or on an open fire at a camp site. Steele used his for roasts, soup and even desserts.

Susan nudged Steeled with her elbow, "Are you going to hold us in suspense forever?"

"Not much of a mystery," added Hardy. "The aroma gives way to the secret."

Steele removed the lid, "My specialty, peach cobbler."

"Eddy. go to my fridge, got some vanilla ice cream. It will compliment Steele's dessert perfectly. You have outdone yourself son."

"I knew it was your favorite Hardy. Of course, if I had known we would be catching the fish for the fry I might have thought otherwise," laughed Steele.

"If you are waiting on me you are backing up, serve it up," grinned Hardy.

Over dessert Eddy asked a question that had been dogging him, "Mister Hardy I delivered posts and chicken wire. Are you planning on getting some chickens?"

"I live off the grid, but I got no notion raising and caring for a flock of narrow heads."

"Then why do you need the posts and chicken wire Mister Hardy. I apologize if you think I am being too noisy."

"You are not nosey lad. It is a fair question considering you brought it out here for me."
"Yeah, I would like to hear this too," added Steele.

Susan raised her hand, "Me too."

"I reckon it is unanimous huh. I did not know that something as simple as buying a few metal posts and chicken wire would stir up so much interest."

"No secrets among friends, right Hardy?"

"You have been paying attention I see Steele. I reckon my business is your business. This is indeed a day of sharing, the past, the present and future endeavors. Coyotes have been showing up way too much lately for my liking."

"Are you going to catch them and pen them up," asked Steele. "I thought people in these parts shot them on sight. There is no season. They are fair game. They have no natural enemies. Getting rid of them is encouraged and expected."

"Trust me when I say it, I have killed my share of the varmints. I hear the packs howling around here almost any given night."

"Now even I am hooked," said Susan. "Just what do you have in mind for those coyotes then?"

"Penning them up is a waste of my time and theirs. My intent is to keep them out."

"Mister Hardy I am no expert on this, but I think you are going to need a lot more posts and wire to keep them off your property."

"Dead right, lad, but I have something else in mind on a much smaller scale."

"You do treasure milking a moment don't you Hardy Bovine, "said Steele.

"Any story worth telling is best told by keeping your captive audience interested. Getting there is an important part of the journey. Yep, I am a certified milker."

"How much milking can you do where fence posts and chicken wire are concerned?"

"All right then. I can see that you folks don't appreciate an old man's sarcasm even with full bellies. I am building a cat corral."

"That's the silliest thing I have ever heard," said Susan.

"Not anything funny about it to those annoying felines that think they own this place," answered Hardy. "Buttermilk and Clabber love the outdoors. Having them roam about in the yard while I am at work has been like ringing the dinner bell. Those ungrateful cats

112

have had more than a few close calls with the coyotes. Cats are usually easy prey. I think those two have used their nine lives and are on borrowed time. They have been nothing but trouble since I made the worst decision of my life fetching them home. I never liked cats. Still don't."

"I am not buying that. If you hated them, you would just let the coyotes get them. You have a soft spot for them, admit it," said Susan.

"I will admit nothing of the sort."

"Then why go to the expense," asked Steele. "And just exactly how do you intend to fabricate this cat corral?"

"Those stupid cats can never make up their minds, inside or outside, outside or inside, ruining my precious time when I am at home. I have been booting them outside while I am working. That's when the coyotes tend to wander in a bit too close, then and when those wild canines wait to ambush them when they feel the need to prowl at night. I pondered what I could do to remedy the situation."

"And your pondering led you where?"

"Like I said, Steele, the cat corral will be a safe place for those good for nothing fur balls when they hanker to be outdoors. Cats by nature are lazy. When it is hot, they look for a cool hideaway to just sleep. When it's cold they find a sunny spot to do exactly the same. Good for nothing I tell you, eating, pooping and sleeping about sums up their sorry lives. If reincarnation is real, I reckon coming back as a cat would be the most peaceful and restful second life anybody could wish for. That is if you can choose living in a coyote free area."

"Mister Hardy I don't get it. It sounds like you hate your cats, but you don't want anything to happen to them. I am confused."

"Me too Eddy, for taking them in the first place…take this as the truth and friendly advice, think twice before you make bad decisions. You must live with the consequences when you stupidly allow better judgment to circumvent your normal way of thinking. If ever you consider owning a pet, get a dog. Never settle for a cat."

"Why Hardy Bovine, I have never heard you refer to Clabber and Buttermilk as pets."

"Slip of the tongue Susan, I was just referencing them as such for the boy's benefit. They are a nuisance, too set in their ways, a might cantankerous, not willing to give ground for anybody."

"Sounds to me like they have learned a lot hanging out with you," said Steele.

"Can we help you build the cat corral Mister Hardy?"

"Thank you for the offer, Eddy. Today is a day for friendship and fellowship and not one for working. Might be you can help me next week with this little project if you have a mind to."

"I would like that Mister Hardy but how does one build a cat corral?"

"Not too complicated, Eddy, I plan to construct a runway from the backdoor that leads into the corral in the yard. They will have food and water, shade and sunshine in that spot. I can scat the cats into the corral and leave them there until it suits me to let them back inside. It will work perfectly when I am away and come in handy when I am home."

"What makes you think chicken wire will keep coyotes out?"

"It works for chickens, Steele. A fence works both ways, keeping things in and keeping things out. I reckon cats are no different than the feathered kind."

"Are you planning to build a roof on this thing?"

"A roof, what are you talking about Steele?"

"Cats are climbers, Hardy. They will be up and over the so-called corral fence before you can say scat cat."

Hardy rubbed his chin, "I reckon this project is going to require a bit more pondering. Eddy I might require more material. Let me think on it and figure what works best."

"Watch yourself Hardy Bovine," warned Susan. "It sounds like to me you are in the planning stages of a cat condo, not a corral."

"This conversation is over," replied Hardy, not interested in debating the construction or the intent.

"Just let me know what you need and when you need it Mister Hardy."

"You will be the first and only one to know Eddy. Some secrets are better kept secretive around this crowd."

"Fellowship with friends during a fish fry is what I recall you saying," Steele reminded him.

"Mind like a steel trap has a way to wear on a person."

Steele, taking a page out of Hardy's book smiled and winked just to aggravate him further.

Mind like a 'Steele' Trap

Hardy gathered his gaggle of friends to the perfect after dinner sitting spot. He had two swings anchored from ancient live oaks. They faced one another making it ideal for further conversation, two people in each.

"Sometimes this is all a person needs, a swing, the peace and quiet and a secluded house in the country," said Hardy.

"Piece and quiet requires solitude, not a bunch of folks disrupting your intent, Hardy."

"I said sometimes. Other times it is a pleasure to share a spot like this with the people that mean the most to a person."

"Are you insinuating we are special in your life," asked Susan.

Hardy mustered a grin and winked, "If I were to leave here tomorrow what will y'all remember about me?"

"There you go again Hardy. You're dying, aren't you?"

"For the last time Steele, I am as healthy as a horse. I don't feel bad. I don't feel sick. I don't have a death wish. I am just attempting to engage."

"Engage my big old butt, Hardy Bovine, you are working an agenda."

"I must agree," added Susan. "This is off even for you. This has not been one of your normal invites for someone not always known for being normal in the first place."

"I hate to pile on Mister Hardy, but you are acting a little weird in a good sort of way. You have never taken us fishing before and never offered to teach me how to clean and cook fish."

"Let us not forget that gar fish and Festus the alligator," added Susan. "This has been some frenzied fellowship on any scale. Why don't you tell us why you really invited us out here?"

"Suspicious minds you all seem to be sporting. I was simply saying that I enjoy living here. Nothing could be better unless I had a cabin on 800 acres, book ended by two mountains and no neighbors."

"Pretend to love the life of a hermit if you want but proof contradicts your pipedreams. If you wanted and enjoyed your privacy you would not tolerate us."

"Are we experiencing just a tad bit of your Sookie persona gal?"

"I'm not Sookie and you sure aren't acting like Hardy Bovine. Unlike you and all this talk about living the life of a recluse, I cannot imagine where I would be today without friends like you. Yeah, that means you too Hardy. Welcoming me into the fold provided me a heart filled with joy. More times than I dare count, this bunch has picked me up when I was down, supported me when I didn't think I could stand. I can always depend on any one of you to give me fresh perspective to face a new day. Y'all have my heart. I love y'all."

Three men stood speechless with reddening faces. Susan had never opened up like this before. They had shared many unspoken moments, but words were never necessary to express true feelings and appreciative interactions.

"See Steele, it is not that difficult," Hardy spoke up breaking the silence.

"See what Hardy? Why don't you stop all this mumbo jumbo and get to your point?"

"Susan has blossomed in our presence, opening up like a morning flower. Even young Eddy has told us things about his health that we could have never imagined. But you, you remain the man of mystery. Never worry about who you might offend by telling the truth. Best you worry about who will be misled, deceived or destroyed if you don't."

"For the record, I am not misleading, deceiving or destroying anybody, especially none of you, by not playing into your silly ass games."

"Look around you Steele. There is always something to be grateful for."

"What makes you think I'm not grateful for everything I have?"

Susan tossed her nickels worth in, "There are two things that always get my days off to good starts. I never watch the news and stay off the bathroom scales. Matter of fact I don't own a set of scales and I watch very little television. Both improve my sanity."

"Having what I got makes it okay not knowing what might come next. I take on every day knowing that whatever it is I can handle it. Time is not promised anybody, especially me but I try not to worry about it. I'm the miracle baby after all. My mother says that waking up is the Lord's way of telling us one more time in His world. It is His wish that we don't squander it and do our best to make a difference. She says that any of us have the ability to touch a heart or encourage a mind or even inspire a soul. She says He granted our waking up so we should respect His wishes and enjoy the day."

"Mighty fine words and a smart mama you have Eddy. See Steele, just another example. You better ease up fretting and swinging like a banshee before you throw the lad from that swing."

Steele ceased pushing off and slowed the swing.

Hardy was not about to let up though. "One day it just clicks. A person realizes what's important and what's not. It begins with learning to care less about what people think and instead focusing on what you think about yourself. You think about how far you have come instead when you thought things would never get better. You

118

find yourself gazing in the mirror and smiling because you are proud of whom you are and have fought to become."

"Where did you learn to psycho babble Hardy? You are too old to be having a midlife crisis. More than likely you are suffering from a senior moment of epic proportions."

"I admit it. I have been a cantankerous fool most of my life, hard to get to know, not a likable cuss from most people's perspective. I always call it like I see it and never mince words. I cannot argue with the perception folks have of me. I laid it out there like an open book. I am not one to apologize even if I might be wrong and I hardly ever am. I can be quite boisterous and unreasonable, especially if someone crosses me or just lands on my bad side. The way I see it, what's done is done. What's gone is gone. Life's lessons are always moving on. There is nothing wrong with looking behind you to see how far you have come but the key to life is to just keep moving forward. Best thing to do is breathe and focus on your strengths and the way you take on challenges. If you are wise enough you will find solutions to your problems and handle whatever needs to be done. Most important, never get so distracted that you fail to recognize and appreciate true friendship."

"Hardy Bovine, you are a piece of work. You have never been this talkative."

"Steele, I used to think that communication was the key until it finally dawned on me that comprehension is. A person can communicate all they want with somebody but if they don't get it, you can't reach them the way you intended. You are a tough egg to crack."

"Why the sudden urgency to focus on me, we have known each other for years. We have always gotten along despite our differences."

"This has nothing to do with not getting along. I respect you Steele Dillon. I just hanker to know you. It is no more complicated than that."

"Now you sound again like a man wanting his last wish granted."

"You boys need to lighten up. You are wearing me out," interrupted Susan.

"I don't know, I kind of like it. What can it hurt, us knowing more about one another," added Eddy? "It's like learning history on a personal level. History has always been one of my favorite subjects. It might be because I may never have a chance to make much history of my own. If anybody here has a reason to ask last wishes you are looking at him."

"What you say Steele, you heard him, grant Eddy his wish."

"Sounds more like yours Hardy, not Eddy's."

Steele did not appreciate the theme of today's fish fry. It was worse than that stupid truth or dare game. He had already had to swallow one shameful moment recently. Pulling that gun gimmick at the shop had been taking matters way too far. Yes, it had been effective but extreme. It had flushed out the perpetrators, but at what cost? His dignity had been compromised and he had no one to blame but himself. He had vowed he would never point another gun at anyone but had royally flunked that promise. It angered him dealing with Hardy's nonsense. Flipside, he felt ashamed not opening up like his friends had. Steele did not like being conflicted. He preferred decidedness. Hardy had forced him to straddle the fence. Friends getting to know friends better had not sounded terrible at first, but this was not the level he had been prepared to go.

Like'em, Love'em, Leave'em

Hardy had proclaimed happy hour had arrived with the meal and dessert now behind them. It wasn't quite five o'clock but close enough according to the song made famous by Alan Jackson and Jimmy Buffet. Hardy offered beer and wine or the hard stuff if anyone preferred it. Eddy had to settle for root beer or a soda of his liking. Both Susan and Steele chose bottled beer. Hardy joined them, Blue Moon being the unanimous choice. Several toasts were made for this and that, mostly friendship related. Each took turns recanting how each of them had met and how long they had been friends, none of which Steele Dillon took offence to. One beer then three furthered the casual stroll down memory lane. The afternoon was filled with sniggering and laughter discussing embarrassing moments as well as heartfelt ones.

"For this most special occasion allow me to break out something that I have been waiting to share for the perfect occasion. This is about as perfect as it gets among the best of the best."

Hardy went inside and returned with a pottery jug reminiscent of what you might see in a movie or television show. He smiled and confirmed it was indeed white lightning. One of the prisoners had offered it as thanks to a situation Hardy had handled preventing the prisoner from being stabbed. Ebb had a friend of a friend, a bootlegger, to deliver it to Hardy. It has been in Hardy's possession for almost four years and had never been uncorked. Today they would uncork the homebrew and pass it around to celebrate a bond stronger than super glue, so Hardy phrased it.

"What about me Mister Hardy?"

"You are underage Eddy," spoke up Steele. "Your parents and the law would have our hides if we allowed you to drink any of that hooch or anything alcoholic for that matter."

"Lighten up Steele. One sip could do little harm. After all, this is solidifying our lasting friendship. Consider it our version of blood brothers and sister."

"Then we should cut our thumbs and commence with the blood rite instead. Giving him a drink is a bad idea."

Susan tossed in her opinion, "I agree with Hardy. One sip can not hurt, one little sip to commemorate our friendship. We are family in a sense and leaving Eddy out does not solidify the bond we have."

"You're both crazy but I suppose I am outnumbered. One sip and that's it. All agreed."

"Agreed," they replied.

"And Eddy, when we say sip, we mean just that. Don't even think about gulping or guzzling or I swear you will receive a swift kick to your backside by my size elevens. Got it?"

"Yes sir, loud and clear. Thank y'all for including me. Not to worry, what happens here stays here. I would never want to ruin what we have. I know I'm the kid of the bunch, but I get it."

"Now that this is settled let's pop this cork and salute our everlasting bond. Susan, you do the honors."

She did and then made a toast before taking the first swig, "May we never stop loving the simple things like fishing, picnics, bonfires and drives down back roads." She then passed it to Steele.

"To the givers, the dreamers, the believers, the doers, the listeners, the forgivers, the trailblazers and to friends caught in the web of forever friendship at a doggone fish fry." He handed the jug to Hardy, but he waved it off and nodded to Eddy.

Eddy took a deep breath, nervous about taking a sip and making a toast worthy of the others. "Here is to a wish for a long life, a chance to do everything dreamed of and to the best friends anybody could ever hope to have." He stuck to his promise and took that sip, one that ended with him coughing and spitting most of it on the ground. Still bent over he passed it to Hardy.

"Mighty fine toast Eddy. Like Susan, I have never found time spent driving down a back road wasteful. And Steele, you spoke volumes with yours. I toast the old ones as being the best ones, old jeans, old movies, old tunes, old time and old friends. One minute you are young and the next minute you find yourself turning down the radio because it is too loud. As friends, if we could look into each other's hearts and understand the unique challenges each one faces, we would probably treat one another much more gently and with greater tolerance. Patience and care come from unconditionally knowing one another and I toast to us being the best we can be to one another given circumstances and secrets shared."

Steele slowly toasted seeing through Hardy and his precise and chosen words aimed directly at him. Maybe he was paranoid, but he doubted it, given Hardy and his pushy ways thus far. He did agree that they had a bond that no one could ever break. He welcomed another pass of the jug. The homemade elixir was doing wonders to ease his suspicions and open his mind. The jug made its rounds a couple more times skipping Eddy.

"I look around here and see two and half men, one woman and wonder why we congregate unescorted, no wives, no husbands, girl or boy friends, just us. Is this a sign of a lonely and sad life? Surely there must be somebody or have been somebody that struck the fancies of those gathered here."
"What are you getting at Hardy?"

"Companionship is a natural occurrence, isn't it? What gives, why is there just the four of us?"

"I don't recall you telling us we could bring someone to the fish fry," answered Susan.

"My bad, who would you have brought gal?"

"I didn't say I would have brought anyone. Just saying you never asked."

"I don't have a girl friend," added Eddy.

"What is your point Hardy?"

"Steele, have you never had a gal that struck a nerve in you?"

"What about you Hardy Bovine? I have never seen a woman on your arm. Never mind, I forgot that you visit…"

"Whoa Steele…"

Susan rolled her eyes. "Guys you must remember that I hang out with bikers. I know about Miss Lottie and what she does to bring comfort and joy. Bravo to you Hardy Bovine."

Hardy wasn't one to be easily embarrassed but his face may have reddened just a tad. "Enough of this talk…"

"You brought it on yourself opening the love can of worms," chuckled Steele. "And no, before anyone asks, I have never ventured to her place."

"I was never the marrying type. And I sure wasn't the 'daddying' type. I avoid women with matrimony in their eyes and never had much use for little snot nose young'uns."

"Tell us how you really feel about the subject," winked Susan.

"No offense gal but it is what it is. I have never been hitched and I am not ashamed to admit it. Never even had a close call either because any woman, present company not included, tends to always want to tell you what'fer and ruin your life once they got their claws in you. I do what I want, when I want and as often as I want without somebody telling me I can't or questioning why I want to."

"I sort of had a crush on Bonnie Faye Turner, but I never had the guts to tell her. Who would want to have somebody like me for a boyfriend? I could kick the bucket at any time. What girl in their right mind would want to gamble on me?"

"I know Bonnie. She is a wonderful girl from a fine family," said Steele. "Look at you Eddy. You can do anything you set your mind to do. Fishing, fighting gators and what woman wouldn't want a guy that can gut and clean what he catches then cook it."

"Eddy, none of us are promised tomorrow. I say go for it, ask her out," said Susan.

"I'm not one to offer love advice but you are not me by a long shot," added Hardy.

"Maybe I will," he smiled. "If I do and she does, my best friends will be the first I tell."

"I've dated a few people but have never had a serious relationship," confessed Susan. "I have always felt like damaged goods. Get your mind out of the gutter Hardy. I mean compromised mentally with what happened to my brother and my mom and the secrets she hid from me. Some days life is just hard living with this package. Riding my bike and working in the shop help me get my mind off it. I guess the thought of a relationship scares me because I don't want to just be liked; I want to be valued for being me. Right now, I am not sure who I am so how can I expect someone else to know who I am. I don't know where I would be without friends like you guys. You always support me and pick me up when I need to be lifted."

"Things take time gal. When you dig a hole and plant a seed it doesn't spout the next day but learn patience because it will poke its head out of the ground. With you, your life will only get better. What I am trying to say is you got to keep working on yourself to overcome the stuff that bothers you. The goodness of the rest will fall into place. When it does you will blossom into the person you were always meant to be."

"You always know the right things to say Hardy."

"Keep that to yourself, might ruin my reputation."

"What about you Steele Dillon? Have you never been married or at least in love?'

The moonshine had loosened Steele's lips a bit and to his surprise he answered Susan. "I have never been married. Best policy is to never allow a woman to steal your heart."

"Like you pointed out to me Steele, I have never seen a woman latched onto your arm either."

"I don't recall you being around 24/7."

"Oh, so is that a yes?"

"It's a no since moving here."

"Then there have been women folk in your past life," winked Hardy. "You're an old Mississippi boy, right?"

Steele nodded.

"Spill it son, any close calls?"

"You are among friends," added Susan.

Steele took another r pull from the jug, "Yeah, friends and fellowship at a fish fry sipping on illegal shine confessing embarrassing moments, what harm can it do?"

"At least you are sipping on that nasty tasting stuff," said Eddy, spitting on the ground to make his point.

"Fine, there was this one little southern bayou belle that might have had a run at me. Her name was Grace, amazing Grace, I often called her. I met her just after I graduated. Mind you, we're going back. We crossed paths on the job. Merely accidental that we ended up working the same shift and we became friends. Friendship led to us dating a few times. It didn't take me long to figure out that she was taking it more seriously than I was."

"You are a man of few details aren't you son."

"Shush Hardy, let him finish," warned Susan.

"Not much more to add, it was in both our interests that we end it. Our jobs were being compromised, end of story."

"What kind of jobs were you doing," asked Eddy.

Steele, squirming like he was sitting on hot coals simply said, "Jobs that were important to both of us."

"Man of mystery you are. You can't even tell your friends what line of work you were in," said Hardy eyeing him down.

"That was a long time ago and doesn't matter much now."

"It sounds to me like you've still got demons out there dogging you boy."

Against his better judgment Steele took another swig from the jug and refused to say more. He had already said more than he intended to say. He had broken one of his personal cardinal rules sharing too much of his before life. Digging up old bones was not his style or intent. Things once buried needed to stay buried. The only life important was the one he was living now. He didn't hold it against his friends for wanting to know more about him. More in this case might be too much. They accepted him for who he was, the Steele Dillon they knew, why chance them knowing the Steele they didn't. While he didn't think anyone would judge him for his past, he saw no value added bringing it into the present. One thing dead on point, Hardy had been right about demons still dogging him, but they were his demons and no business of anyone else, including the three people he trusted the most.

"Susan, is there anyone out there that you wished you would have treated differently like Bonnie in my stupid life?"

"If I must be honest there was this one guy, but he doesn't live around here. Me taking a do over isn't possible I am afraid."

"Why, do you not know where he lives now?"

"More complicated Eddy, he's married. And before you guys get the wrong impression, he wasn't married when he lived in this vicinity."

"Did he get hitched to get over you breaking his heart," asked Hardy.

"No, there was never a 'me' to get over. Eddy and I have that in common. I never divulged I was interested. I thought about...a lot, but I never summoned the courage to tell him how I felt. Snooze and you loose."

"Sad bunch we are," said Hardy shaking his head.

"Why are you feeling so sad old man? You said you didn't want to marry or have children. Sounds like to me that you got your wish."

"I was feeling sorry for the rest of you. Y'all are young enough for second chances. Even if I had a change of mind my time has come and gone. Time is precious. Y'all best not squander it."

"Thinking about dying on us again," said Steele.

"For the last time for Pete's sake, I am not planning any such thing. The Lord might have another notion but that's His choice not mine."

"I hope He has another choice for me Mister Hardy. I for one know exactly how precious time can be."

"Lad, life for any of us is never perfect. Best we can do is make the most of it and as many memories as we can and don't let anybody steal our happiness. Never make apologies for being you and doing what you want to do. Look where it got me. I am still kicking and expect you to live a long life as well. I hope I am around when you tell your story of how you licked what you are going through and it becomes somebody else's survival guide. No matter how your story ends never let it be written that you gave up."

Eddy smiled and nodded his approval. Susan fought back a tear, thinking about what Hardy had said and how it impacted her life. Even Steele was taken aback by his words. Hardy briefly thought about that dang Elrod Long.

Regretfully Fretful

The moonshine continued to work its magic. Had this been by design or mere chance? Eddy was the only one exempt from its pull. He didn't require the liquid courage to be openly frank. Faced with illness in his life he had nothing to hide from his friends. Susan had paced her drinking. She had learned to sip not guzzle when around her biker buddies. Her way had always been to remain in control. She never wanted to be the one wondering what she had said or done the day after. Susan preferred being the observer and sober enough to make sure that those that had overindulged got home safely. Steele uncharacteristically had taken the bait, a conduit to possibly opening up. It was not Hardy's intentions to get any of his friends drunk. He just wanted to get to know them better and was willing to toss out any of his personal dirt if anyone was interested.

"Well, I reckon we can close the door on our love life. Opening that can of worms didn't expose anything off the juicy scale."

"We are not exactly the wild bunch," laughed Susan.

"For somebody like me when the end finally comes, it won't be the years in my sorry life that counts, more the life in my years more important. As I have grown older, I realize how precious life can be. I have less tolerance for drama, conflict and stress. It is all about having great friends, a cozy home place, food on my table, and being around folks that make me happy as a pig wallowing in mud. You must be careful who you let board your boat though because some are apt to sink her just so they can be the captain. Some friends pretend to be friends."

"According to you Mister Hardy I thought it was nearly impossible to sink a pontoon."

"He was figuratively speaking Eddy," clarified Susan.

Eddy shrugged.

"Shifting gears, do any of you have any regrets? I'm not speaking of little bitty run of the mill regrets. I am talking about the big'uns, them what might have been game changers if you had done it differently."

Eddy rubbed his chin and brought up Bonnie again.

"Here we go again," barked Steele crossing his arms in protest.

"Steele, surely even you have been dogged by something that you either did or didn't do that. if given the opportunity, you might have done it another way or not done it at all."

Steele sighed and stood from the swing as if taking center stage. He kicked the dirt and then rubbed his hands through his hair. "Dang it, Hardy Bovine, you are a persistent old devil aren't you. I get it. We are friends. This bunch is more than just friends. And yeah, friends should be able to talk about anything without hesitation or remorse. It has not been my intent to clam up while the rest of you have been an open book. Sorry, I have never been one to share personal business. It is personal for a reason."

"Steele you don't have to say anything that makes you feel uncomfortable."

"Hush up gal. Let him be," said Hardy. "Go on Steele, what's got you all worked up son?"

"Back in Mississippi, I was a cop. I wasn't a cop long but long enough, too long."

"Wow, you were a policeman," said Eddy.

"Yeah, Eddy I was a policeman. Kids hope to be this or that when they grow up and my dream was always to be a cop. And before you ask, there were no cops in my family. I was the first and only one."

"Do you still have family in Mississippi?"

"I do Susan."

"Dang it, gal, hold your inquiries and let the boy speak his mind while he has the notion to."

"As soon as I was old enough, I enrolled in the police academy. I was in hog heaven, learning the ropes, doing what was required to be what I always wanted to be. Didn't take long to realize I had found my calling. I was good at it. My superiors knew it too. I was one of those overachievers, the best of the best. I'm not bragging just stating fact. I breathed the blue and all it stood for, living the dream. I was partnered with K. P. Walsh. We took the streets like category five storm, intent on making our town better than we had found it. There was no place for lawlessness in bayou country. We did not disgrace the badge. We did everything by the book. If we arrested somebody you could bank on it they needed to be arrested. Evidence justifies incarceration.

There is something unsaid between partners, complete trust, knowing that each can count on the other in any given situation. You learn each other's strengths and weaknesses. None of us are infallible. Circumstances can change in the blink of an eye, and we must act on gut, but within the parameters by which we have been trained. Mistakes can be costly. And there are certain lines that must never be crossed. Cops are humans. Humans make poor decisions. My partner and I crossed a line that we shouldn't have. Did I regret the choice I made? I did afterwards. My partner did too. Did having regret prompt us to undo what we had done? Nope. My partner and I took being partners to a new level. We fell in love. Taboo, you never do that with your partner. I was smitten by Kellie Elizabeth Walsh. The feelings were mutual. She was my true and only love."

"I thought you said her name was Grace, the girl you fell for in school," said Eddy.

"Puppy love, yes Grace was amazing. I just tossed her out there to get Hardy off my back. Kellie and I were the real deal and from a work ethic perspective, it was wrong from the get-go. That's why we kept it under wraps, no hanky panky on the job or out in the open.

We took great care to conceal it. What we should have done was request new partners, but we enjoyed being partners. So much for me being the model cop. I knew better but it did not stop me, did not deter us.

A racial incident blew up in town. All hands on deck, the entire force was called to control mounting tensions. We were sitting atop a powder keg. Protests quickly turned to a full-blown riot. Fires and looting prevailed. Cops and firemen were being attacked by both sides. It is nearly impossible to stop gang looting. Believe me we tried. We had hoped to bring it under control but there were those with political aspirations stirring the pot. Cops were deployed to protect the instigators whether they wanted us there or not. You have seen it play out on television too many times. Our small town was on the national stage. The catch phrase 'Mississippi burning' had never been truer.

After several days things started dying down a bit. Maybe the perpetrators had run out of businesses to burn and loot. Whatever the reason, we welcomed the relief. While the town resembled a burned-out shell of a war zone, at least life was returning to normal for us cops. Kellie and I had returned to our regular patrol and areas that no longer resembled our normal beat. We spotted a man walking down the sidewalk with a television. He was struggling to hold it and maintain his balance. We sounded the siren and flashed the lights. He stopped in his tracks. It was odd behavior because usually they drop the merchandise and haul butt when we have them cornered solo.

We asked him his name and he gave us one. He said he was taking the television to his uncle, saying it had been a loaner. Kellie asked him to set the television on the sidewalk and show us some identification. He eased it down and reached for his back pocket. We both had our hands on our weapons and warned him to take it slowly. He did as instructed and had the wallet in his hand. I asked him to hand it to Officer Walsh. He offered her the wallet. Just as her fingertips touched it, the wallet fell from his hand and like a flash he pounced and had her around the neck with a knife to her throat. We had dropped our guard and it cost us dearly. He then drew her service revolver and demanded that I drop mine. I refused. He then walked Kellie backwards, her gun aimed at me, the knife still to her throat. I attempted to talk him down, but he hushed me immediately.

Without warning he fired her gun at me prompting me to duck and roll behind our cruiser. When I gained my composure and chanced a peek, Kellie was lying facedown in the grass and our perp was gone. I called for backup as I headed for her. The grass was stained crimson. He had slit her throat. Try as I did there was no saving her. She was dead and the bastard was gone. I held her in my arms until the medics arrived knowing that there was nothing, they could do for her. The wallet contained no identification, just twenty-seven dollars. I'm not sure why he even carried it. A search of the area came up empty. They did later find her discarded gun, but prints had been wiped clean."

"Dang son, that had to be a tough pill to swallow."

"It gets worse. I was on desk duty until everything panned out. Kellie was dead and I mourned her death as a partner not a lover. I returned to duty but losing a partner is not something you get over easily, especially when the partner was much more than a partner. I was a broken man, but I was still a cop. I had been drinking more than I usually drank but I never drank while on duty. I never drank myself into a stupor either. Bar hoping was an escape. I mostly went through the motions just a way to escape the loneliness. About three months later I was in a bar when I saw a familiar face. It was the bastard that had murdered Kellie. Here I was, off duty and there he was within ten paces of where I sat. I guess he realized he was being watched. Sometimes you can just sense it. We made eye contact and then he bolted out the door. I followed and caught up with him in an alley that dead ended.

Cornered he pulled a knife, most likely the same knife that he had used to kill Kellie. I told him 'Not this time' and eased closer. I asked him to drop it but of course he didn't. Why would he? I removed my leather jacket and began swinging it as a buffer. He lunged and I managed to entangle his arm in the jacket, and I wrestled the knife from him. Now I had the knife and the advantage.

134

He held up his hands giving up. I had her murderer, justice about to be served. I then buried the knife in his gut. The shock on his face was priceless. I pulled the knife out and stabbed him again and again until I backed him against the wall. I continued to plunge that knife into his lifeless carcass. When he fell to the ground, I wiped the knife clean and then placed it in his hand chuckling 'suicide.' There wasn't anything funny about what I had just done though. I had done the unthinkable, the inexcusable.

The next morning, I turned in my shield and gun offering no explanation beyond I was not cut out to be a cop. I walked away from my dream job, a cold bloodied murderer. I was no better than the scum that had killed Kellie. I regret losing her and losing the job I always wished to have. I do not regret doing what I did though no matter how many times I tried to convince myself it had been the wrong thing to do. Justice had been served by me. Who better to serve it? I had not done anything close to that until I brandished the gun at the shop the other day to flush out those who had damaged my truck. The difference though, I did not intend to use it. Still, it brought back a flood of memories. I regret using that tactic on my coworkers."

"Are you a desperado Steele? Are you here because you are outrunning the police?"

"No, Eddy, I am not hiding from the law. Matter of fact I was asked to view the body to see if he might have been the one that had killed Kellie. Seemed he had stabbed another woman when he had attempted to rob a store. I told them it wasn't him. I am a murderer and a liar. How does the session feel now Hardy? You have allowed the worst of the worst into the fold of friendship. I killed that man and then walked away from everything. My father ran a small shop back in Mississippi. I worked in it and learned the trade as a kid. After I left the force, I helped him for a while but there were too many bad memories in my hometown. One day I just packed up and eventually ended up here. I call my parents occasionally, but I've not been back, and they don't know where I live. It is best for everyone."

"Steele your past doesn't impact how I feel about you," spoke up Susan. "That man murdered your true love, and you settled the score. I could have done the same thing as a mere twelve-year-old had I known back then that my brother had been murdered."

"I was a cop. A good cop and I knew right from wrong. Times had changed though. As fast as we would catch offenders, they would be released back on the streets just to do something more heinous. I feared that her killer would get off on a technicality. I had no proof to connect him to her murder other than me being there as a witness."

"Son, you had the knife. Bet it was the same one he used on her."

"Blink of an eye you must make a decision. I wanted him dead. I must live with that decision. Rage and revenge are powerful emotions. Toss in the loss of the only person you have ever loved, and the end game isn't pretty. Just like when I placed that gun to Clay's head at the shop. Rage and revenge got the best of me. Those boys should never have messed with my pickup."

"But you didn't kill anybody," Hardy reminded him.

"But I could have had I not taken the time to think it through and get Red on board."

"What happened at the shop?"

Steele waved off Eddy's question thinking vigilante justice again. "I need some fresh air."

"Boy, lest you have forgotten, you are outside where it is fresh as a daisy," said Hardy. "Just take a second and breathe it in."

"I need some fresh air alone," he said as he walked toward the river.

"That went well," said Susan.

"I never would have figured him for a cop," added Eddy. "He is a bad ass."

Hardy regretted having pushed his friend so hard. It hadn't changed his opinion of Steele Dillon, but he now fretted for his wellbeing. A fleeting thought, he wondered if Steele was his real name or had he concocted an alias. He just as quickly dismissed the premise. The boy was only running away from himself not the law. That is unless he had lied about how it had played out. His gut told him that Steele had told the truth. His eyes hadn't lied. This had not been something easy for him to share.

Susan broke the silence asking, "Do you think one of us should go check on him?"

"No gal, he has to work through it. We would just muddy the waters. I might have handled the situation exactly like him given the circumstances. I have always been a firm believer that if you pick a fight, you make dang sure you win."

"That man picked it for him threatening Steele with a knife," said Susan.

"No, Steele picked it as sure as we are standing here talking about it. He was a cop, and he could have called for backup even while off duty. His loss clouded sound judgment. He knew exactly what he was doing once he decided to go down that path. It was not going to end well for one of them. That feller had committed murder and he dang sure knew that Steele was the cop that had witnessed it."

"Why didn't he just stop once he had possession of the knife?"

"I'm betting he has asked that same question plenty of times, Susan. Or maybe he never intended to allow the feller to live. This is just another fine example of why I stay clear of serious relationships. Once bitten, it clouds your perspective. You are no longer in control; they are. Worst still, you feel obligated to defend and protect them. Toss young'uns into the equation and all bets are off. Now you got them to protect as well. Your life is kaput. It belongs to them. I didn't make it to where I am by making stupid mistakes like falling in love or worse, getting married."

"Maybe I better rethink my feelings for Bonnie Faye Turner. I don't want to end up in a pickle like Steele."

"Eddy, don't allow this to cloud your judgment. There are no similarities," advised Susan. "And shame on you Hardy for saying what you said."

"Mister Hardy, you said we all seemed to all get along and see things the same way," added Eddy. "Besides, my days might be numbered. I am probably the last person that should be looking to get involved with somebody."

"Don't talk like that Eddy. Tell him Hardy."

"The lad has got to follow his own gut. It is neither for me nor you to tell him how to live his life gal. I would be mighty ticked off if anybody tried to tell me what to do with mine."

"This is just fine Hardy Bovine. You started this and now you just want to wash your hands of it. Eddy this is not a time to be worrying about it. Good and bad things happen in our lives. Best thing to do is to keep living life to the fullest and not stress over what you can't control. God has the wheel when it comes to any of us living and dying. It is what we make of it while we are here. As long as you breathe you are strong enough to handle all challenges, and you are smart enough to figure out solutions to what life tosses at you. You can do anything you set your mind and heart to do."

"Susan, it sounds like to me that you are figuring out your own path," winked Hardy.

"I know how easy it is to be hard on myself. I have traveled this road plenty of times. Most days life is hard if you let it be. Other days it is rougher than you think you can survive. Some days you must give in to it and cry before you can move forward, and this is okay too. My world crumbled when my brother vanished. I regret I didn't do more to find him, but I was just a kid too. I also regret not realizing what a toll it took on my mother until it was too late. It has been a tough thing for me to grasp that life is not mine to take. It is all about the giving too. It isn't just blindly seeing. It is felling as well. Those feelings can be good and not always bad. It's not all about hearing, it is about listening. Life is not settling for just existing. Life is about living. Frank 'Crawdaddy' Crawford and Wiley Fritz opened my eyes to what can be and what can be accomplished if you set your mind and heart to it. It doesn't mean that I don't have my fair share of struggles and setbacks. You, Hardy Bovine, have impacted my life for the good too but it doesn't mean you can't royally piss me off with how you treat people, especially your friends. There is no excuse for abruptness. Sometimes you need to think before you spout hurtful nonsense."

"Dang it, gal, don't hold back, say what you mean. I reckon eating crow is not good even when seasoned to make it go down better. I regret I have gotten on your bad side."

"You are still missing the point. You have no regret about what you said just the reaction you received. I know, you say what you mean and mean what you say. Well, sometimes choosing your words more carefully can better get your point across."

"I'm too old to be changing my ways. I am what you see and what you get, no sugar coating it to spare fragile feelings. If can't handle the truth it is best you stay out of the conversation."

"See, I rest my case."

"Are you two mad at one another?"

"As a wet hornet would be the way Hardy might phrase it."

Aren't you forgetting about Steele?"

"Thanks, Eddy, for putting things in perspective," said Susan. "I was just going Sookie on Hardy and for that I do apologize."

"You got no reason to apologize to me. I am the one that owes my friends an apology. I fanned this fire and allowed it to break free into a barnburner. I reckon we should all go check on him."

Where There is a Will There is a Way

Steele sat on the riverbank and skipped rocks across the water. He had never intended to venture down this path. They now knew the truth. He was a brutal murderer and an accomplished liar to boot. He was a false friend if ever there was one. Maybe it was time for him to move on again. Realistically though, there was no sure-fire way to outrun your past, not one as daunting as his. He had allowed himself to fall for his partner and he had breached cop protocol and had broken one of the Ten Commandments, 'thou shall not kill.' How could he ask God to forgive him when he could not forgive himself? There were too many years behind him to even be thinking this way. Now, his very best friends knew who the true him was. They would never view him the same nor would he expect them to. He had made his bed.

He realized that it had first begun coming unglued when he had pulled the stunt at the shop. Once done, he relived the stabbing. The aftermath of the emotions had been quite devastating. To compound the issue, he had no one to talk to about his feelings. Hardy had meant no ill will with his prodding today. He knew that now. He had just wanted to be a friend. True friends should have no secrets, at least none as dark as the ones he had been concealing. Then why didn't he feel better? Confessions are supposed to be good for the soul. Others now knew he had committed murder and had covered it up. It had not been fair, him burdening his friends with this knowledge. One or all of them might feel obligated to turn him in. He certainly would not blame them if they did. If they didn't, they would have to live with the same burden as him.

"What a mess you have made of this," he whispered.

"No mess. Today you have become the person you were always meant to be, Steele. That never could have happened had you not relieved yourself of the baggage. Leave it in the past son. You have a chance to start over with us by your side. What's important is that you learn valuable lessons from bad things. Forgive yourself of those mistakes and move forward. We are here to help you heal," said Hardy.

Steele stood and turned to face Hardy, Susan and Eddy. All were smiling and stepped forward to embrace him. Even the tough old bird Hardy Bovine joined the spontaneous group hug.

Hardy stepped back and offered more words, "On this road called life you must learn to take the good with the bad no matter how bad the worst can be. It's not always easy to smile when you are sad and forget love that has been lost. Remembering what you had doesn't always heal a hurting heart. It is a tough row to hoe, forgiving and forgetting when things go dreadfully wrong. You are caught in those crosshairs but understand this Steele, people change, and you have already changed for the better. Your ride is not over. It is just beginning. You got us to ride along to make the ride smoother."

"I don't deserve friends like you."

"It is we that don't deserve a friend like you," said Susan. "You laid it all on the line and you did it because of our friendship. There is nothing that you have said that has changed how I feel. We might not hurt like you have hurt, but we feel just the same and we love you Steele Dillon. That is your real name, right?"

Steele laughed, "Guilty as charged."

"You are the baddest ass I have ever known," said Eddy.

"Present company not included," added Hardy.

"Come on folks, let's go have a seat. I got something I need to say. No, I don't have bodies buried out here; none that I am willing to confess to just yet."

Everyone took their seats in the swings except for Hardy. All that was missing was a podium according to the posturing he was doing. He cleared his throat more than once folding and unfolding his hands. It was obvious that whatever he was about to say was not going to be easy for him to spit out.

"You're dying, aren't you?"

"Dagnabbit, I wish you would stop saying that Steele. You say it enough it is apt to come true and I am not in the mood to die today."

"Do you need me to pass you the jug?"

"No gal, I don't need any liquid courage for what I need to say. I am trying to do what you advised me to do and think about what I wanted to say and how I wanted to say it before I say it. The old dog is trying to improve with age."

A Rite to be Right

Hardy Bovine was a complicated individual by any measuring stick. He had survived hard times and tough situations. He had always kept his business private, less factual and had never been a braggart. Had old age softened his hardboiled persona? Probably not but he had recently stepped back and taken a long look at what had been. He hankered for the first time to give those he cared about a glimpse at some of it. He wasn't sure how willingly he was ready to become an open book though. Some things were better off not said or relived. When he looked back on his life he felt the painful moments, too many mistakes and a handful of heartaches. When he looked at the feller staring back at him in the mirror he saw a glimmer of strength, harshly learned lessons, and a sense of pride for mostly doing the right thing by people who had ventured into his life.

He thought about some cowboy logic, not that he was anywhere close to being a cowboy. It was mostly just stuff he remembered reading some where of no particular importance. He pictured the image of a trail worn and weathered old cowpoke with captions like *while on this ride called life you got to learn to take good with the bad, smile when you are down and out and love what you got and never forget what you might have had. Try hard to forgive even when it is tough to forget. Learn from all those sorry mistakes but never let the regrets rule you.* Hardy recalled that one last saying, people change, things go wrong but the ride goes on. Cowboy wisdom was powerful mantra. They never fretted over how educated, talented, rich or cool they were. Integrity was framed by how you treated people. Sometimes Hardy wished he had lived in another time, maybe the old western frontier. He had never owned or ridden a horse so what made him think he might have made a fine cowboy? More his style was he watched people and their actions, figuring that if he did, he would never be bamboozled by their words.

Now he sat among his closest and best friends trying to muster up the spit to quench his parched throat and lips to say what he wanted to say. What he had to say was not earth shattering. It wasn't a life changing prophecy either. Everyone has issues, and because of those issues people have a story. Growth is nothing more than a dance. All people dance to a different song, to a rhythm that suits them to a tee. Growth is not a light switch that you can turn off and on. Even in his thoughts he felt like a babbling old silent fool, often making perfectly good sense while other times being lost in the dang weeds. A sergeant once told him before they were about to go into battle that it was okay to be confused because it was just another way to learn valuable lessons. He told him that it was perfectly acceptable to be broken because being so is where you begin to heal. Frustration promotes decision making. The sarge added that in sadness you learn bravery if you listen to your heart and latch onto the wisdom being tossed at you. Remember to be worthy and finish the job you started. Back then he just figured it was war time banter to help those never exposed to the horrors, a distraction from its cruelty. Odd how stuff embedded deeply surfaces when you least expect it.

Hardy wondered if he was stalling spending all this time thinking. To him it felt as if he had been pondering for quite a spell but in reality, he hadn't. It wasn't like the others were just sitting there staring at him wondering if he had drifted into old timer's world. He certainly was not one for making speeches, but he had unfortunately laid out this grand plan to speak the words appropriate for the situation. The situation was an odd way to frame it. Well, he reckoned it was all on him, not them, not just yet anyway. It was way past time to get off the pot and just let her rip. Procrastination just led to stammering and stuttering. When he spoke, he wanted it to come out precise and deliberate, not that of a babbling old fool. What he had to say was important. Well, it was important to him. He had no feel for how they might accept what he had to say. Best to just get it done and say it and quit the over thinking.

"I reckon y'all have figured out that this was more than just a good ole southern fish fry. I had a rhyme to my reasoning for asking you here."

"Dead giveaway when there was no fish to be fried," said Susan.

"Yeah, mighty odd to invite us to vittles and then we must hook our own or go home hungry," added Steele.

Eddy just shrugged, "I had a blast fishing and fighting alligators. I got to meet old Festus."

"I do apologize for misleading you folks. My way is not always the best way to get things done. In my head it can tend to be clear as a picture but to others it is fuzzy, out of focus. There is such a thing as over thinking and I reckon I am guilty as charged."

Steele was growing impatient again, "Hardy, why don't you cut to the chase and spit it out. What you got to say does not have to be polished and precise. We are big boys and a girl. We can handle and process whatever you toss at us, even if your days are numbered."

"Last time, stop pushing me into a grave. I am a long way from being a cadaver, ready for the coroner or the funeral parlor. Both feet are firmly planted above dirt and that's the way I plan to keep it for as long as the Lord will see fit. I might ought to ask you if you are dying Steele. You certainly seem to dwell on it more than the rest of us."

"Sorry, and no I am not dying that I know of either."

"Me either," chimed in Susan.

"In my case I never know," smiled Eddy. "If I am there is not a whole lot I can do about it, so I just don't think about it."

"Have mercy! Now that this has been settled can I just say what I need to say?"

Steele rolled his eyes, "None of us are getting any younger, have at it Hardy."

"Let me just start by saying that what I am about to say it not something that I have dwelt on for a long spell. I mean, it is not something I have fretted or stressed about. It just happened and it is my obligation to share with you folks since it involves you."

"That cleared up everything now didn't it," spoke up Steele.

"Steele, you might practice listening a mite more than yapping all the time. The Lord gave you two ears and one mouth for a reason. Just saying."

Steele pretended to zip his lip and bowed offering Hardy the floor again.

"Now for the record, this was not my idea. The seed just got cultivated and had no choice but to see it through. Well, I reckon I had a choice but once it got planted it got rooted and once it got rooted, I had to nurture it. Well, I didn't have to but dagnabit I did. It latched onto me like a tick on a hound. Shoot…what I mean is…well, it don't matter much what I mean…what's done is done so there!"

"You have said a lot for not saying much. I thought you had taken the time to think about what you wanted to say and how you wanted to say before you offered to say it."

"Susan, I am older, not necessarily wiser than all of you. You must remember I have lived to dial a rotary phone and share a party line. I have listened to music on phonographic records and eight track tapes. I had a black and white television before Technicolor was invented and I fine tuned the reception with rabbit ears and tinfoil. I spent most of my life not taking pictures of myself like is done today. When we did take a selfie, we stood in front of the mirror and aimed the camera at it then we had to use up the roll of film and get it developed to see if the picture took like we hoped it had. I played hide and go seek until it got dark and made my toys from paper and wood. If not for our vivid imaginations, we would have been bored out of our gourd. We played army, cowboys and Indians before all the politically correct nonsense ruined good harmless fun. Sorry, once a babbling old fool always a babbling old fool."

"And we are no closer to whatever it is that you want to tell us. Certainly it isn't strolling down memory lane with you," said Steele. "Or maybe it is. Do you want the jug now?"

"No, I don't need the jug. I just need you to focus and listen."

"It will be much easier for us to listen when you decide to focus," rebutted Steele.

"Opinions don't define any of us so you can stop pegging me for someone I might not be."

"Saying you are not focusing isn't exactly pegging you for anything," replied Steele. "Just tell us why you wanted us all here today."

"Yeah, Mister Hardy, just having a past is a good thing. I sure hope to have a long past I can look back on," said Eddy.

"If there is something dreadful in your past, be assured that we will not judge you for it," added Susan. "The past cannot be changed. It is what it is."

"Everybody has a different journey. Sometimes things improve with time."

"Hardy, please stop talking in circles and just make your point. Stop over thinking whatever it is you are thinking."

"Steele, I am getting there. As we age certain things change about us. Sometimes I tend to forget someone new name ten seconds after they tell me. I find myself buying too many vegetables then tossing them before I eat them because they go bad. I hate digging through the trash for a box that I need for cooking directions. I wash clothes then put them in the dryer and forget to get them out and they end up more wrinkled than they were before I wadded them up in the first place. Don't get me wrong; getting old is still a blessing and beats all alternatives but a man has the right to change how he thinks on things, right?"

"I don't think there are any rules to govern how one thinks or changes one's mind. Are you having a late life crisis or something?"

"I don't know Steele; maybe. One thing for sure you tend to view things differently, for good or, in some cases, bad reasons. Sometimes it isn't even your idea in the first place. I am not one to dwell on such poppycock nonsense as fighting with people, hating others or being petty with whatever time I have left on God's good earth. Peace of mind is what's important and choosing how you hope to leave this world."

"Hardy Bovine, you don't get to decide how you leave unless you take your own life. You aren't going to do something stupid are you?"

"Gal, you know I am not the cowardly kind. I would never consider doing something like that. Dang it, this is getting way off track."

"Well, you're engineering the train. We're just passengers. Blow the whistle and tell us what you want to tell us."

"Steele, I am getting there at my own speed and my own way. My life has been a bit shy on perfection. I have never been married. Matter of fact I don't recall ever having been in love. I never had one of those bucket lists and I still think having one is a foolish notion."

"There you go talking about dying again," interrupted Steele.

"There is nothing wrong with talking about dying Mister Hardy. I do it all the time. It makes you stronger. Don't get me wrong; I want to live a long time, but I am not scared of it. Worrying about it doesn't make it go away. You got to live while you can and for as long as you can without doing foolish stuff. Everyday I wake up is a good day. My preacher says that we should always remember that we are in fellowship with God. If we do, we don't have to worry about anything. He says God will care and provide everything we need while on our personal journeys. He says when our mortal body is finished on earth, he has a new one waiting for us in heaven. It is a win win for us. I reckon I can use this one for as long as He grants me then get my new one when He decides I need it."

"Eddy, you are wise beyond your years, and it is my honor to call you my friend," said Hardy. "The Lord is indeed the provider. Sometimes we tend to forget that, all caught up in our trials and tribulations. Those scientists profess we need four basic things to survive, water, air, food and light. For once they are dead on. The Bible tells us that Jesus is the Living Water, the Breath of Life, the Bread of Life and the Light of the World. I am not all that religious but there is nothing wrong with believing what makes perfect sense."

Eddy smiled, feeling the same about those gathered here this afternoon. Friends forever, however long God granted them the time.

"Mighty biblical of you just the same Hardy," added Steele. "Are you about to preach a sermon or get to your point?"

"Sounded nice to me," said Susan.

"I am far removed from living my life in a Godly manner. I do read and I do listen even if I stray off the path best followed from time to time. What I have got to say has nothing to do with my regrets from living my life my way. I did it. I own it. I cannot undo any of it even if I wanted to, which I don't. I live for today and do it the way I see fit. There is nothing wrong with thinking about tomorrow. A man must be a complete idiot if he doesn't plan ahead. You don't want to walk into surprises if you can help it. One of my worst failures is that I don't always limit my thoughts to just when I am alone and instead tend to let the wrong words fly when I am with people, too opinionated and set in my ways to change now I reckon. Too many wrongs cannot be righted, not that I have a notion to fix them."

"Sorry, this still sounds like a last will and testament to me."

"I am beginning to think you have a death wish for me, Steele."

"Nobody should ever have a death wish," spoke up young Eddy. "Hoping for a long life is what everybody ought to be thinking."

Susan placed her hand on his shoulder and explained, "It's just a figure of speech between those two. Neither of them really means it Eddy."

"Please accept my most humble apology lad."

"Yeah, it was way out of line and inconsiderate of us," added Steele.

"Hey guys, I am not that sensitive about dying. We all do it, remember. Some of us live longer than others, that's all. I don't hold against anybody saying stuff like that or living longer than I might. I don't like people saying stuff like they wish they would die, or they hate their life. That's just me though. I got my reasons for seeing things differently. Everybody else has theirs."

"How did you get so smart lad?"

Eddy just smiled as Susan gave him a big hug.

"Sorry for interrupting Hardy. Please say what it is you have a mind to say."

"Thank you for granting me that sincere blessing Mister Steele," winked Hardy.

"Friends, fellowship, fish fry and tomfoolery, you got it all covered, don't you Hardy Bovine."

"One thing you tend to figure out if you live to be my age is that the grass isn't always greener on the far side of that fence. And you can't always find happiness by moving from one place to another hoping the next one will be your happy place. You can't really mend a broken heart if it isn't worth fixing in the first place. Heavy burdens must be totted even if you don't think they are worth the effort. In the long run happiness is what you make of it. Nothing much else matters, at least not to me."

"Hardy, have you found your happy place or are you still searching for it?"

"Fine question there Susan but my happiness has nothing to do with it. Everybody has a different kind of happiness. Sometimes it makes sense to others. Sometimes it doesn't. A person can look like they are living a miserable life, but it might be the life they have chosen to live. It might not be what another person might pick but that's what makes us different. They say the Lord made us the way we are and that we are not supposed to be like somebody else. Trying to be like somebody else goes against His wishes for us. We got nothing to prove to anybody until we are willing to prove it to ourselves first. Yep, Susan, I am happy and content with the life I have lived and am blessed to still be living. Nothing is perfect. It was never meant to be perfect. One man's right might be another feller's wrong or visa versa. It doesn't make anybody better or worse than the other. It just makes us different and followers of other paths. We have just as much right to be wrong as we have the right to be right. Some folks have a tough time latching on to that concept, always judging people by the standards they set for themselves."

"Dang it, Hardy, you have no short responses today, do you? A regular chatty Cathy you are and a philosopher to boot. Something has changed you. Hopefully we will figure it out eventually if you stop being so long winded and vague."

"Being long winded and vague are gifts for an old coot like me. Some folks my age would be mindless old babbling and drooling fools."

"You have the babbling part down pat. The drooling can't be too far behind," chuckled Steele. "I suppose it is your right to be right, right? I just wish the old Hardy would emerge and not be so wordy and get to the point."

Guns and Ashes

Words are just words. Some are more important and powerful than others. Saying what needs to be said isn't always as easy as said. Hardy Bovine was all but choking on his word selections, the words that really counted right now. Talking points are worthless if you can't spit them out. He had all but talked his friends to death, wearing them out while he traveled in circles, not making much sense in the big picture. There is no value in getting to a point if you can't get to the point. Some call them talking points. His were far from it, more pointless so far. No, that was all wrong. Everything he had said he meant but without getting around to saying what he meant to say in the first place.

Anticipation of their reactions was just a boat load of undetermined what ifs. They were his friends, his best and most loyal friends, possibly his only real friends; why wouldn't they abide by his wishes. Steele would go off half hinged thinking he was right along, that last wishes were those of a dying man. He must thoroughly convince them that he was not a walking dead man, not that he knew of. There is nothing wrong with planning ahead. People do it all the time. It takes the guess work out of other folk's hands. Nobody else should be burdened with what should or shouldn't be done in case of the worst possible conclusion. Any sane person would want to make their own choices in matters that might upset others to make. Who better to know what was right than yourself? Then why was he struggling to spit it out. He was the furthest thing from being a procrastinator. Getting it done was his mantra. It always had been. Dilly dallying was just a sorry excuse by any measure. There was no time like the present to remove the dilly from the dally. Put up or shut up. Say it and get it behind you. Take you medicine like a man. All these thoughts were just a load of crock. Elrod Long was to blame for his troubles and current dilemma. Elrod Long was not here and putting this off on him was too far removed now. Hardy Bovine now owned it for all practical argument.

Steele Dillon had been his first real friend. That was a sad admission given the long life he had lived so far. There was no need arguing with the truth. He had allowed very few folks to get close to him. It wasn't by design. It was just how things were. Maybe it was his reclusive ways when not at work. He could get along with most anybody unless they crossed or riled him. He was not a people person, but he tolerated people better than a lot of folks. He and Steele had this connection. Might not have been an immediate one but it hadn't taken long for their friendship to blossom. Steele was a no-nonsense straight shooter like him. Well, shooting straight had been lost in translation lately, him choking on what he wanted to tell Steele and the others. Hardy recalled the very moment it all clicked, and he realized Steele would be more than a passing acquaintance. He had dropped by Red McClain's Fabrication Shop, needing someone that could weld a busted trailer axel he used for hauling his pontoon. Red introduced him to a new feller that had recently started there.

Steele Dillon had followed him back to his place and had done a fine job repairing the trailer. Jawing while sharing some time it became obvious that both shared similar views of the world and life in general. Steele spotted some other needs around Hardy's place that could use the skills he could offer. Steele did this in a manner that was neither intrusive nor insulting. It was his matter of fact way of putting things that Hardy warmed up to, feelings that caught him by surprise. A friendship was developing, one that neither had sought out. Both kept their personal business close to the vest and each respected that fact, neither of them asking questions that were none of their business. If something needed to be said or shared it was left up to the person that wanted to say or share it. It was then and only then that the conversation might progress one way or the other. Until today he had no idea that Steele had been a lawman nor the incident that had driven him from that profession. He had more respect for the man now.

Steele had been the conduit for bringing Susan and Eddy into the fold. A woman and a kid of all things; how unlikely had it seemed that those friendships would blossom as well. Hardy would not take anything for the bond they had developed. He was certain the others felt the same way. Digging in these holes was getting him no closer to where he needed to be. It had been his pick to do it today over any other day he could have chosen. Again, procrastination was not his normal approach. He had already laid the foundation, each of them opening up to take the pressure off him. Why did he perceive this as pressure of any kind? This was not a life or death situation. Well, it had some relevance but not to the extent that Steele thought. He hoped the young lad did not take his revelation the wrong way. The boy was wise beyond his years, why would he? Susan had experienced her share of hard knocks; death being front and center much of it. Certainly, she would appreciate the importance of his decision. Listening to what he had to say was one thing. Understanding and accepting the logic behind it might seem a little squirrelly. He would never belittle any of them if they had any last wishes or requests. His weren't that far fetched, were they? Part of it was common practice, personal choice. He had just added a bit of edginess to his. Might be that they would revel in the unique innovation in getting it done. Friends sharing and participating was not that farfetched. It happened all the time. No better time than It was time for the rubber to meet the road and just tell them what needed to be told.

"Steele, Susan, Eddy I reckon I have been stringing this thing out long enough."

"You think! You are just now noticing," replied Steele. "You've been floundering worse than one of Eddy's fish."

"Hardy, I must admit it as well. You obviously have something on your mind, and it seems like you think it could jeopardize our friendship if you tell us. I assure you that there is nothing you might say or do that will break the bond we have."

"What Susan said," added Eddy.

"No denying it gal, I am not worried that what I have to share is going to adversely impact our friendship. What I am about to impose might unleash unfair pressure on my dear friends. It is not my intent to make any of you uncomfortable with what I have not been comfortable in saying."

155

"For heaven's sake Hardy, just get it off your chest and let us decide how we feel about it whatever the heck it is," Steele encouraged him. "Let me guess. It has something to do with this Elrod Long fellow."

"What do you know about Elrod Long?"

"Rest my case, that certainly got your attention, didn't it?"

"Who is this Elrod Long? I have never heard you mention him," said Susan.

"Me neither," said Eddy.

"It's because I have never mentioned him," said a frustrated Hardy.

"Confession, I heard you mumbling earlier almost cursing the gent under your breath. And no, I was not eavesdropping. You were talking out loud, loud enough for me to hear you."

"Dang that Elrod Long..."

"Yep, that's about what I heard you say."

"Did this Long character do something to you? If so, we're here for you," said Susan.

"All in," added Eddy.

"Just tell us how we can help you Hardy," said Steele.

"Tarnations, this has nothing to do with Elrod Long; not directly. Well, maybe a little but he had no say so in what I decided to do."

"You have an uncanny ability to talk in circles today."

"I admit it Steele. This is not my normal way of handling a situation. This isn't just any normal situation though. And if you point your finger at me again saying I am dying, I am apt to toss you in that river as a meal for old Festus."

"No need getting your feathers all ruffled at me. I am not the one acting a might peculiar today."

"Point taken; I apologize. It seems I am doing that a lot today."

"Not nearly enough with what you have been putting us through," rebutted Steele.

"Dang it, son, you make me sound like I am a cantankerous old fool."

"Most days you can be but today you are a chapter too hard to read."

"You know me. I have never been an open book."

"Not until today but something has caused you to rip back some pages. You have done a nice job getting us to do the same. Me reluctantly, I might add, but you did it all the same. You have your reasons. We're just waiting for you to share them with us,"

"Oh man oh man, sometimes it is best to keep the worms inside the can."

"Are we going fishing again Mister Hardy?"

Hardy winked at Eddy, "I reckon it will be me dangling the bait and hoping I catch what I set out to catch."

Eddy shook his head not understanding what Hardy meant. Susan rolled her eyes, wondering how whatever he had to say would play out. Steele continued to eye him suspiciously, certain that whatever he had to say would impact all of them one way or another. He was not about to bring up dying again though.

"All right, here goes. Elrod Long is neither an accomplice nor a threat. He is just an inmate that I play checkers with over at the prison. Like any game of checkers there is plenty of friendly discussion. Most of it amounts to nothing. The inmates are stuck in their world so how much value can they really add to ours. It was a checker game like any other checker game. Like I said, most of the conversation doesn't mean a hill of beans. I leave what is said there after I go home. I never dwell on any of it. They did what they did to land themselves inside and there is nothing I can do to help them or change what they did. Mostly they never talk about what they did or how they feel about it. They accept their life as the way it is and do their time until they serve it out or are pardoned. That dang Elrod Long just had to up and say something that stuck a nerve with me. I didn't think what he said had bothered me until I arrived home. Against what I usually do I dwelt on what he said. The more I dwelt the deeper I got into it."

"I hope you are not planning a prison break and wanting us to help you. See, I said nothing about you dying."

"And I am too old to serve time for attempting a prison break. None of them are worth it anyway."

"Sookie might be in, but Susan enjoys life the way it is. There is no means that justifies that end as far as I am concerned."

"I am trying to be serious and y'all done sidetracked me."

"Seems to me that you are easily sidetracked and distracted from what is really on your mind," replied Steele.

"Try hushing up and give me my few precious minutes? That goes double for you Steele Dillon."

Steele stifled a comment and just nodded. Susan and Eddy confirmed that they understood loud and clear.

"Elrod Long messed up everything. He started jabbering about wills and how everybody needed one. I didn't pay him much attention at first because I really don't have any next of kin to leave anything to, so I figured why worry about it. What happens when you buy the big one? Dead is dead but what do they do with you once you've croaked. I had always figured that this was a no brainer. You die, they dig a hole and plant you, not much more complicated than that. I reckon there is a bit more to it like picking a coffin and having someplace to stick you. Truth, I have never figured it would be somebody else's problem. With no kin who would be making these decisions on my behalf. No, Steele, I am not sick or on my death bed."

"I didn't say a word."

"You had that stupid look on your face. I've seen it too many times already today. I got home and couldn't shake the notion he had planted, what to do about a will and how I would want to be laid to rest. The notion latched onto me something fierce and wouldn't turn loose. When I need to work out a problem I do it best by writing it down. The bad thing about touching a pencil to paper, once I do it is a done deal. No eraser can undo my thinking. It's like I have my foot stuck in a bear trap. I cannot get out. I must see it through until I have the answers I need and an action plan worth following. The more I scribbled the more George Dickel was getting quite friendly and on a work night of all times. I had put the dying part ahead of any thoughts of a will. Sorry, Eddy, I didn't mean it the way it sounded. I wasn't trying to choose a way to kick the bucket; I was trying to figure out what would happen after I bought the farm.

I know it sounds morbid but thanks to Elrod Long I was trapped with no way out. I jotted down my options. One, I just let the undertaker bury me. If I did, I either had to pick out a coffin or just let the undertaker use whatever one fit. Second option, I could be cremated. Chills ran down my spine thinking about being set fire. Stupid I know. When you are dead you can't feel so fire isn't going to hurt. Just the thought of being reduced to a pile of ashes didn't set well. Then again, it should be cheaper to cram you inside a bottle than what a coffin probably cost."

"Urn," said Steele.

"What did I say?"

"You said bottle."

"Urn, bottle, jar, what difference does it make? Maybe I would want them to put me inside an empty Dukes Mayonnaise jar. Wouldn't that be a hoot?"

"Is that what you scribbled on that paper?"

"No Susan, I didn't write down Dukes then. It just came to me now."

Eddy added, "I haven't thought much about what happens after I die. I figured my parents would oversee it."

"No need to dwell on it, lad. If God be with you that won't be happening anytime soon."

Steele's curiosity had gotten the best of him, "So what did you decide, Hardy, traditional or cremation?"

"Dang it, Steele, can't you just let me tell it my way?"

"Your way might never happen at the rate it is going. Sorry, please proceed."

"I didn't research the cost of either, but it just seemed to me that that urn must be cheaper than a big ole coffin. I had no idea what the going rate was for turning you into ashes versus filling you with embalming fluid. Did one offset the other? I wasn't really thinking about the price to plant me. I was more focused on the how to instead. You hear stories about people getting cremated and their ashes anchoring the family mantel, or the ashes being sprinkled in the ocean or someplace that meant something to the dearly departed. If I chose cremation, I didn't want what was left of me placed on display like some cheap carnival sideshow. Besides, who did I know that would want me on their mantel? I reckon my ashes could be scattered on the river, but the practice seems too normal and overused. I'm Hardy Bovine. I want to go out in style. George Dickel and I thought on it a spell longer and came to a decision. My wish is to be cremated."

"And this is what you have struggled to tell us," said Steele.

"It's nothing to be embarrassed about Hardy," added Susan. "People decide to be cremated all the time."

Eddy spoke up, "I have never known anybody that has been cremated before. I mean, I really know you now and when it happens, you will be in one of those urns or maybe a Dukes mayonnaise jar. How cool is that?"

"Hate to be the bearer of bad news, but my ashes are not going to be stuffed inside one of those urns nor a jar. It hit me like a bolt of lightning, but I wasn't sure at the time if what I wanted could be done. It's my body and my wish but is it something an undertaker can do without it being against the law or against their ethical judgment. If my Uncle Tom was still here, I could have asked him. You see, Uncle Tom was a mortician until he got busted operating an illegal tattoo business at his funeral home. He's dead and buried. I ran my idea past a couple of local undertakers and neither one of them flinched at my request. It was a done deal then as far as I was concerned. Next, I needed to make a will so my last wishes would be included and known once my day came. My recorded last testament includes everything anybody needs to know about what to do when I have bought the farm. It is legal and has been notarized. I'm good to go."

"And this is what you have been dragging out," questioned Steele. "Great, you have a will, and you want to be cremated. Join the millions of other folks that have blazed the trail ahead of you. Thank you for sharing it with us."

"There's more to it than that, Steele. You are listed as my executor. I hope this doesn't pose a problem."

"I'm surprised but I suppose I can honor you proudly unless I go before you do. I hope you listed a backup plan, someone else off the bench in case of."

"If you go before me, I will find somebody else. Nobody mentioned that I needed to list a bunch of bench warmers. I don't want you to be caught off guard by what I put in the will so I thought you should get a heads up. After I am cremated, I want my ashes loaded in shotgun shells."

"Shotgun shells?"

"Do we each get one Mister Hardy? That would be cool to have you in a shotgun shell."

"Eddy, that's a little morbid," added Susan.

"Why, those urns end up in people's houses, why not shotgun shells?"

"Well said lad, but I have something else in mind that I believe you will like even more. After I am cremated, and my ashes loaded in twelve gage shells. I have listed some of my guard friends, Hubert Wilson, Skipper Pinson and Willy Sprigs, to have the honor of shooting my ashes, firing them over a parcel of land I own in Summerville. If there are enough shells to go around, I would like each of you to fire a round; that is if you want to do it. Keep taking turns and firing until you are out of Hardy Bovine ammunition. I bet nobody else has ever had this done."

"That is out there even for you Hardy," said Steele.

"I disagree. It sounds exactly like something you would come up with to me," smiled Susan.

"I sure hope I am around to shoot you," said Eddy.

"Shoot my ashes lad," Hardy corrected him. "There's more though. Like I said, Steele you oversee making sure everything listed in my will comes to pass. After today I will probably be making a few adjustments in my final bequeathing. Susan, if I don't outlive those dang cats will you take them or at least see to it that somebody puts up with their endless peskiness?"

162

"Hardy, you have more lives than the nine given those cats. I suspect you will be here long after they have used their last ones. If you don't, I will take them in."

"Thank you, gal, I knew I could count on you. Eddy, you get my pontoon and all my fishing gear. You earned it fair and square today."

"Chances are you will outlast me too Mister Hardy."

"Nonsense, you are a walking miracle, and something tells me that the Lord has other plans for you yet."

"I hope you are right."

"Hardy Bovine is never wrong and if he is he never admits it," winked Hardy. "That brings me to you Steele Dillon. I am bequeathing you that parcel of land where my ashes will be scattered and this little place here. Sell it, barter it or do whatever fits your fancy because it won't much matter to me when I am on the other side of that dirt."

"Why me? Why do I deserve your house and land?"

"I didn't exactly say you deserve a 'cotton pick'in' thing. Somebody needs to get it and it might as well be you. You don't like cats and while you enjoy fishing every once in a while, wetting a hook belongs to young Eddy. I got no other close friends so seems reasonable that you get it. Maybe you will find a little filly and settle down here and make some baby Dillons or something before your seed gets too old to sprout any."

"Lot for me to live up to don't you think?"

"I'm done thinking. These are my last wishes and come Monday, I will make them legal and binding. All y'all got to say right now is much obliged, I do, or I don't want them. Not to pressure any of you but I don't have a backup plan for who gets what. And Susan, there

163

will be a little in the kitty for you taking care of those dang cats. If the cats go first, my last will and testament will say you get the nest egg just the same. Eddy, I will add a little extra for you in a trust fund. Steele, yours is all in land and memories of this place."

"Thank you, Mister Hardy. I will cherish the fishing stuff."

"I'm not dead yet and you are welcome to use it all you wish while I'm above dirt."

Susan hugged him to acknowledge her acceptance. Steele remained quiet, trying to absorb what had just happened. This was supposed to be a friendly fish fry, not something filled with revelations and morbid endings. He still wondered if Hardy was holding back something concerning his health. He was sounding more and more like a dying man than one thinking he had plenty of life left in him. He eyed Hardy up and down trying to read his body language, anything that might show the hand he was playing. Hardy was offering no glimpses if there was something there.

Hardy thought this had gone better than anticipated but was not satisfied because Steele had refused to comment so far. He was trying to read him and was coming up with blank pages. No doubt, this had been a lot to unload on his friends but waiting had not been an option. He needed to clear the air now and know where they stood with what he planned to do. Two out of three had offered no resistance. The one left standing was a tough egg to crack though. Elrod Long had gotten him into this mess and the convict was not here to give him moral support not that there was a moral bone in the worthless varmint. It was just him and Steele so what would the verdict be on his last wishes. Hardy figured this should be a no brainer. Steele came out smelling like a rose getting pretty much everything for nothing. Take a few Hardy shots in the air and then what was left belonged to him other that what he left Susan and Eddy. Why then was his friend stonewalling? Just take it and be grateful. Honor an old friend with his last wishes. It wasn't any more complicated than that.

"Steele, say something dagnabit!"

Steele took a deep breath and then did the unexpected. He turned and walked away a second time. Being speechless was one thing thought Hardy but turning your back on another man was just plain disrespectful. The heat was rising in Hardy Bovine's face. He did not appreciate this sort of attitude from his friend. What kind of nonsense was Steele pulling? Did he want the pontoon? Lord forbid he had a hankering to have those two cats. Had he unknowingly insulted him? Whatever bug was up his butt he needed to let it out and air this thing before it got any worse than apparently it already was. Hardy watched as Steele made his way toward the river. What was he going to do, throw himself to old Festus in some sort of tantrum or protest? None of this was making any confounded sense.

As if on cue, Susan said, "If he wants your cats, it's okay with me."

"I hope he isn't mad because you offered me your pontoon Mister Hardy."

"My wishes are my dang wishes, and nobody gets a say so in them but me."

Steele was nowhere in sight now. Had he really jumped in the river? This had gone off the rails big time thought Hardy. Was the will or the thought of shooting his ashes all over the place?

Until Death Do Us Part

Steele had followed a game trail along the riverbanks edge, a different route from his previous exit. He needed time to digest what Hardy had sprung on him. Being an executor was one thing but expecting him to accept his land and home was something else entirely. He had his own place and didn't need the responsibility of another homestead and all this land to boot. Hardy Bovine should have asked him first, but he wasn't the type to ask anyone's permission to do what he had his mind set on doing. Shooting him all over the place inside shotgun shells was about the craziest notion he had ever heard, but no denying it, it was pure Hardy Bovine. And now the mystery behind Elwood Long made perfect sense. Why had Hardy allowed this Elrod Long's opinions to influence his own thinking?"

Steele wondered if the time would come when he found himself standing in Hardy's shoes. Everybody was going to die sooner or later. His partner had not had the time to plan hers, knifed in the blink of an eye. Retribution had been served by his hands but killing the killer had changed nothing. She was still dead. Until now he had not pondered on what her last wishes might have been. She left no will behind and it wasn't his business to make decisions for her. They were not married. Her parents had the last word on the arrangements, just a simple funeral and burial except for the police protocol in the ceremony. Death, he surely did not like thinking about it or dealing with it, thank you Hardy Bovine.

Young Eddy sure deserved the fishing gear and pontoon. That boy was a fishing prodigy. Steele hoped Eddy would live long enough to enjoy them. Thinking such foolishness sounded like he was wishing Hardy to die so that Eddy could enjoy them. What was the real chance that Hardy might outlive Eddy? Hardy was a crusty old soul while Eddy had the deck stacked against him. Hardy had certainly lived a long life filled with whatever he wanted to do. Eddy had so much yet to experience. Losing either friend anytime soon did not set well with Steele. This dying business had not been in today's cards, not to him. It was supposed to be a friendly fish fry. Hardy had snookered all of them. It had been a set-up from the get-go. Plus, he had pried into their personal business under insincere pretenses. Why was it so important for him to know about their personal lives just to spring this on them? Something stunk to high heaven and getting to the bottom of it was the only way for Steele to come to terms with this awful mess.

Steele almost felt like he had taken the cowardly approach by running out on his friends without so much as a word to explain his intentions or concerns. He needed to think on it before he could discuss his feelings. Wrestling with it on his lonesome was not getting him any closer to act on that notion. Steele had broken code by first getting revenge for his partner then by reconciling the wrong at the shop. Backsliding had been more worrisome than he had let on to Hardy earlier. Now this, it was almost overwhelming. He had agreed to be the executor of Hardy's will before Hardy had dropped the other shoe. He wasn't begrudging what Susan nor Eddy had coming to them once Hardy kicked the bucket. They were both true friends if ever there were any, but why had Hardy done this to him? Steele had almost lost track of time but, he had only been walking less than ten minutes on the trail along the edge of the river. He heard a loud splash and caught a glimpse of something disappearing below the surface. He wondered if old Festus might be stalking him looking for an easy meal or just revenge for what had happened earlier. Nonsense, that old alligator was not capable of thinking revenge just because Hardy had been a damn fool naming it. The families of the fish caught today should be the ones seeking vengeance if there were any to be had. Who was the damn fool now, thinking such foolishness?

"You better clear your head Steele Dillon and resolve what has got you in this fix," he whispered.

Having a conversation aloud while alone was not exactly the characteristic of a sane person. Steele paused and bent over grabbing his knees while sucking in some fresh air to hopefully clear his head. It was then that he heard the others calling his name. What must they be thinking? He had never acted like this around them before. He had always been levelheaded, cool, calm and collected. Thank you,

Hardy Bovine, for prying free deeply embedded memories. Hardy had his Achilles heel, Elrod Long, and now Steele had his as well named Hardy Bovine. It was a terrible feeling, allowing someone else to plant seeds that sprouted roots in a blink. Steele's cage was royally rattled just as sure as that Elrod Long had rattled Hardy's.

He should probably answer the calls from his friends but instead Steele took a seat on an old cypress log. Sweat dripped off the tip of his nose. He was tempted to let out a banshee cry to free some of the frustration but doing so would probably scare the others. He stifled the inclination instead. One thing for certain, he could not hide in these woods forever. Stupid thought, he was not hiding. He just needed some uninterrupted quiet time to think. He would never be able to it with Hardy expecting him to acknowledge his wishes. Accepting responsibility for being executor was one thing, but he had never expected Hardy to leave him the farm and start him to thinking as well. Beating a dead horse does not make the horse deader. The voices were getting closer. They were hunting for him. Hardy was like a bloodhound, probably trailing him. He could not avoid the inevitable forever and it was not fair to his friends him acting like this. He finally yelled to them to stay where they were, he would be there in a minute.

Fact, Hardy would die one day. Fact, if he outlived him, he would abide by last wishes, like it or not. There was more in play than just Hardy's will now. Steele wasn't sure he was ready to enter a confession chamber just yet. All of them had confessed too much already. What happens among friends best stay among friends. He was not worried that it wouldn't. They were all trustworthy to the core. One might think you could not trust a kid to keep their mouth shut but Eddy was no normal kid. He was an old soul if ever there was one. Susan believed in the code as well, loyalty and friendship trumped everything. Hardy Bovine, say no more. What troubled Steele, had to be said sooner or later.

The Trouble with Telling the Truth

With darkness creeping in, Steele approached the area where he had deserted the others. An impressive bonfire was burning, and a single figure silhouetted in the foreground. Time to face the medicine, Steele sighed as he slowly walked in the direction of the fire. The person turned and faced him. He could not make out the expression on Hardy Bovine's face. He mostly wore a poker face anyway.

"Where are the others?"

"Gone," replied Hardy. "Eddy needed to get home. He was Susan's passenger. Both were concerned about you. I told them not to fret, you would be fine. You are fine, aren't you Steele?"

"Fine is a matter of perspective."

"Try me then. I am quite the expert where perspectives are concerned."

"You are full of it and surprises, no denying that."

"That's what I have always liked about you Steele. You speak your mind like I do but this is different."

"Well, who made it different; not me."

"Just spit out what's stuck in your craw. Didn't that walk you took do anything to straighten out your perspective? I do my best thinking walking this place or just taking a ride on the river. Clears my head and makes me see things in ways I might not have seen them otherwise. Sometimes I can remember the phone number from my childhood, but I can't remember the password on one of my contraptions. When you reach my age, one minute you're having flashbacks of those days when you were young and bullet proof then in a blink you find yourself turning down the stereo in your vehicle to improve your eyesight. I have learned a couple of valuable lessons in my old life. I don't recall the first one but the second one is I need to always write things down," laughed Hardy doing his best to lighten the mood.

"I see through you like looking through a window Hardy Bovine. Make me relax; drop my guard to loosen my lips. You have sure had your way today, haven't you? Some fish fry I will say again, coercing your friends into confessing their sins or hidden secrets."

"True friends should have no secrets,"

"True friends would not use trickery and guilt to con their friends into telling them."

"What, I'm the bad guy here? It seems to me that everyone here fostered some relief laying their worries and secrets on the table. Look what Eddy faces daily. Now we can feel his anguish and help the lad when he finds himself in a dark place. And poor Susan, tough row she has hoed, losing her brother and mama under awful circumstances. Look at what you went through, and you relive it more than a person should ever have to do it. Regrets, remorse, what ifs, they are all the same. They are important and worrisome but when our number comes up and our time is done on earth, none of those things really amount to a hill of beans. Same goes for money or material things. What really counts is how we treat other people, those that we love and cherish. It will shine and live on forever in the hearts of those that were impacted."

"Amazing, Hardy Bovine almost sounds like he has this sentimental heart. What makes you think you are suddenly an expert on these matters and gives you the right to be so intrusive?"

"I don't see it like you are framing it. I did not make any of you say a dang thing that you didn't want to say. If you hadn't wanted to you would have kept your mouths shut but you didn't. What was inside needed to escape and where better to turn it loose than among friends."

"That's the way you see it, huh? Whatever Hardy Bovine wants he gets, and he feels he deserves it at all costs."

"What is really eating you Steele? You sound so angry. That anger is telling you where you feel powerless. You sure have a mess of anxiety bottled up. Your dang anxiety is letting you know that something in your life is out of kilter. I smell fear on you too. Fear is a powerful tool. It let's you know you care about something or somebody. All these bottled up feelings you got are not random acts. They are messengers. You got to listen to them though. They are trying to tell you what you really need or what you need to do."

"There you go again, the expert on everything thinking you have the answer for what ails us. Who made you our lord and master? Sorry, you voted yourself the head honcho in what matters to those around you."

"Is it the will? If you would rather not be the executor of my dang will then just say so. There won't be any hard feelings. When I made it out, they told me that somebody needed to oversee it. I could not think of anybody better suited to see to my last wishes. I reckon I should have run it by you first instead of unloading it today thinking you would be all right with it. Assumptions can land you in a heap of trouble if they don't go as you assumed that they would."

"I am fine with being the executor. I said so a while ago, didn't I?"

"But did you really mean it? Maybe you walked it off and decided differently."

"If I said it, I meant it Hardy."

"Then what has got you so worked up? I'm not dead yet and I am not planning on going belly up anytime soon."

"Hardy Bovine always thinks he controls everything, including dying."

"All right, I get where you are coming from; I got no say so over when I go unless I do something stupid to get there sooner."

"Hardy, dying is your business, not mine. I hope you have plenty of good days ahead. I really do."

"I believe you Steele, but it still offers no explanation for what has got you all worked up. It's just me and you, speak what's on your mind. You know what they say, if bacon hasn't solved your problem, you didn't cook enough bacon."

"Hardy, I am humble enough to know that I am not better or smarter than anybody, but I am smart enough to know that I am different than most people. You see things your way and I see things my way. Sometimes we are never going to see things eye to eye."

"I'm not a turnip that fell off the truck. I know that. They say that money can buy a person a house, but it doesn't necessarily make it a home. Money can buy you the best bed, but that bed might not make you sleep any better. You can even buy the best clock, but it won't give you more time. Money can buy a book but not the knowledge to make you smarter. Money can buy you all the food you need but it cannot give you the appetite to eat. Some think that money can buy friends. It can't, no more than it can buy love. Everything that I am leaving after I kick the bucket isn't buying me anything. Hell, I won't here to see it through. That's your job if you still want it. What I'm doing with this will has no strings attached to it. I don't expect any of y'all to get all teary eyed and say what a wonderful feller I was. I don't give a rat's butt if you say anything at all. What I am asking has no hitches and it isn't complicated. I own stuff and the stuff needs to go some place. I figure it might as well go to ones that meant the most to me while I was alive."

"I appreciate the sentiment and I'm sure the others do too. Like I have said, I don't need anything you have but I understand why you are doing it. It has to be done or somebody else will just decide what to do with it, most likely a public auction."

"Then what else is there to this than that Steele? I'm just divvying it up and trying to act responsibly when the day arrives. Elrod Long made me think about it, to plan ahead and take that worry off others.

I regret he did it but I don't regret acting on it once I realized it was not a bad idea."

"I get all that and we have beat the dead horse bloodless."

"Then why did you wander off like you did? You must be thinking about something."

"Yep."

"Yep, that's it, just yep."

"You know me Hardy; I am not one to open up. You worked hard to pull my past from me, my life as a cop and what happened, what I have done my best to forget and leave behind. Confessing to it opened a flood of emotions, the last thing I expected to confront as this fish fry. I have worked hard to fix myself, patch up what has been broken. It hasn't been easy, not by a long shot, using crazy tactics like talking to experts, reading up on it in books, try this plan and that. It has not been easy to get to where I am and now this."

"Steele, has it ever crossed your mind that maybe you don't need fixing. You could have falsely latched on to the idea that you needed to be fixed. You can't force homework on yourself when you might just need to let it go. You cannot change what happened and it will drive you squirrelly if you keep blaming yourself."

"I know that."

"We're friends and you have a shoulder to lean on if you have a mind to. I'm not one of those head doctors, not that I am saying you need one, but I am a mighty good listener and got plenty of opinions and advice."

"I have tried therapy."

"Not Hardy 'by God' Bovine therapy you haven't."

"It's not what you have done, it's the will."

"The will, I'm not following you."

"I don't have a will and have never thought about having one until today. Thank you, Hardy Bovine and Elrod Long."

"Why is having a will troubled you so?"

"It's the premise of making one that has gotten under my skin."

"It really isn't as complicated as it seems. I did it didn't I."

"To you maybe."

"If you're hankering to make a will I will help you, it's old hat to me now"

"Not so simple even with your help."

"Trust me Steele if I can do it anybody can."

Steele shook his head, "I need to get out of here."

"What's your hurry? It's not a workday tomorrow and besides, aren't you the foreman now? And don't tell me you are a church goer."

"What if I am, is that such a bad thing?"

"Being foreman or a church goer?"

"I need to head home."

"Steele you really need to work on not being so stressed and focus on how blessed you are."

"Thanks for your hospitality. Don't you go dying on us anytime soon."

"If I do, you will be the first to know," Hardy smiled and winked. "And if you change your mind on making out a will…"

"Goodnight, Hardy."

Steele watched in his rearview mirror Hardy still standing by the fire as he drove off. He almost regretted leaving things like he had but he was not ready for all this will talk. It required serious soul searching and not off the cuff discussion. Hardy's heart was in the right place, but his heart wasn't in it. The man had done what was right for him and he had done a fine job of it. He appreciated the thought Hardy had put into the planning and leaving what was important to him to those who were equally as important. All of that was fine but beside the point as far as he was concerned. You could not go from no will to a will in the blink of an eye.

Steele's mind was racing on the drive home, but his speedometer was doing anything but reflecting the urgency in his thoughts. He was barely maintaining the minimum speed limit on the back road. He seemed to do his best thinking when his hands clutched the wheel of his old truck. It was his prized possession, something built from scratch by his two hands. He had salvaged it, saved it from becoming just another rust bucket. He saw promise in what most thought was a junk pile. Beauty was in the eye of the beholder, so went the saying. That's why he had taken it so personal when those jokesters at the shop had desecrated his creation. A fleeting thought, if something happened to him and he still had her, who would he trust her with? That dang will thing had raised its ugly head again even when he was not trying to think about it. Nothing much else that he owned meant anywhere close to what that truck meant to him. That was just it; nobody would ever appreciate her like he did.

That Elrod Long had started this whole mess putting the idea in Hardy's head. What did Hardy have to do; drag the rest of them into it. Not fair, he had not heard Eddy or Susan cry foul over what Hardy had laid on them. Only he had allowed it to get to him and for the most obscure reasons. Reasons just the same, they were his and only he could work through it. No therapist, including Hardy 'by God' Bovine could cure what weighed so heavy on his heart and mind. It wasn't complicated so had said Hardy and it really wasn't that complicated unless you had your reasons to make it complicated. Steele wondered if he was making more of this than he should, but it mattered and what mattered was that he had no solution for it right now. He didn't want to think about it but not thinking just made him think more.

He reacted quickly, almost on instinct, braking and swerving simultaneously to miss the huge buck standing in the middle of the road. Easing the truck to the side of the road he firmly planted both hands on the steering wheel and rested his forehead against it too. Thinking about that will had almost cost him his beloved truck. He knew better than to allow his mind to wander while driving. His world had always been one guided by discipline. He first had taken matters into his hand's vigilante style at the shop and now this. He was slipping royally, allowing emotions to rule him. Bad things happened when he allowed emotions to take charge. People got killed or almost killed. Knowing the difference between right and wrong became blurred. If he hadn't confided in Red McClain what he had wanted to do to flush out the scoundrels responsible for damaging his truck he would probably be occupying a jail cell now. Red had given him the nod to give it a try. It had gotten ugly but had thankfully worked.

Steele fired her back up and again headed homeward. Nothing of worth would be settled tonight. He thought about what Hardy had said, asking him if he was a church goer now. He wasn't. He had even blamed the Lord years ago for his partner's death, knowing even back then that He had not caused the thug to knife her. He thought about what a therapist once told him. 'You might not see it today or tomorrow, but you will look back in a few years and be perplexed and in awe how everything that happened to you, large and small, brought you somewhere you needed to be. One day you might even be thankful that much worse things didn't happen and it all worked out for your better interest.' None of that had made any sense then. The jury was still out for now. One day, not today and probably not tomorrow, he would tackle making a will. He didn't want his parents burdened with having to make these decisions after the fact. He had a sudden urge to call them; maybe not tonight, but maybe tomorrow. Steele took a deep breath and cleared his head as best he could and finished his commute without any additional drama.

Lock and Load, Ready, Set, Fire

It was a cold and blustery day today having been in the seventies just two days prior. In the south if you don't like the weather just give it time and it will change one way or the other. This time it had changed for the worse. A cold front was approaching, bringing plenty of wind and rain. Downpours were in the forecast by noon. The darkening skies indicated that the local meteorologist unfortunately might get it right this time. Nasty weather any way you viewed it.

Steele sat inside the funeral home's parlor, not comfortable with his role but promises made were promises kept. It had been almost six years since Hardy Bovine lured them into to that fish fry. Now it was time to abide by his wishes. Steele was the executor of Hardy Bovine's will, and it was his honor to follow everything his friend wanted down to every detail as screwy as they might seem to those just hearing them for the first time. The funeral director had complied with them as well, saying he thought he had seen everything now. He smiled adding that he admired the new twist and appreciated the thought Hardy Bovine had put into it.

The service would be simple as Hardy had asked for it to be. Well, the burial portion of it would be anything but simple. Firing someone's ashes, loaded in shotgun shells, was raising the bar for spectacular and unpredictable. Only someone like Hardy could think up something like this. Steele was taking his responsibilities seriously for his old friend, more so than he had accepted the premise years ago. The weather was a downer but then again, so was Hardy if you thought about it. Thunder and shotguns being fired would be the perfect Hardy storm.

They arrived at the parcel of land in Summerville. With Hardy's shotgun in hand Steele asked who among them wished to take the first shot and honor the man's last wishes. Present were Hubert Wilson, Skipper Pinson and Willy Sprigs from the prison, none of them stepping forward to volunteer. Susan, seeing that none of them were going to man up, raised her hand and said she would. Steele gave her the look, are you sure? She caught what he meant and nodded. Steele handed her the shotgun.

"Before we do this, I think it is fitting that we say something to acknowledge Hardy Bovine. He picked his gun totting pallbearers for a reason. He either liked us or respected us for being good shots. Hardy Bovine accepted me as one of guys after Steele Dillon brought me into the fold. He always treated me with the utmost respect and never addressed me as Sookie, only Susan. I was present at the fish fry when he told us what he wanted us to do after he moved on to his final resting place. He also encouraged me to find closure for circumstances that had haunted me for too many years. I owe him a lot and will forever miss his friendship and kindness. For Hardy Bovine I fire his first round of ashes to honor a man that would be here firing any of our ashes if he had the chance."

With that Susan aimed the shotgun tilting it upward slightly and fired the first shot across the long stretch of open field that once belonged to Hardy and soon would be Steele's. She smiled and then turned to Steele and held her hand out asking for another shell. "Let everybody else get their shot before we shoot any extras."

"Steele, this one is not for me. It's for Eddy. Remember, he was the one who said he was looking forward to shooting Hardy."

"Yep, I remember. Hardy corrected him telling him he was not going to be shooting him just his ashes. Here you go. Fire one for Eddy."

Susan loaded the second shell but before firing the gun said, "Eddy learned to fish, to battle garfish and even fend off a surprise encounter with Festus the alligator. That day over six years ago Eddy cleaned what he caught and cooked it with perfection. He enjoyed many more times with Hardy and us on the river and at Hardy's home. Eddy helped Hardy build that hideous cat coral that has survived the test of time and the rebellious cats that were corralled inside it. No matter how it looked, it served to be coyote proof. Eddy Southard lost his battle with leukemia two years ago. Like Hardy, the loss left a huge irreplaceable void in our lives. Eddy, this one is for you." Susan said as she fired the second round.

She handed the shotgun to Steele. They shared a hug before Steele popped in another shell and then asked, "Okay boys, the lady has shown you how to do this. No time for shyness."

Skipper Pinson held out his hand and retrieved the shotgun. "That dang Hardy was about as worthless as they came. He was always playing checkers with Elrod Long and treating the prisoners way more respectable than they deserved. That was Hardy Bovine. He treated everybody equally no matter if they were a worthless criminal or a worthless guard that tended to them. Go, Hardy. Spread your sorry butt one last time." Skipper fired the shotgun toward the open field. "Have a restful life old buddy."

Hubert Wilson shook his head, "What in tarnation made him think up something this crazy? I would have figured him for the in the ground type, not cremation and certainly not loaded inside shotgun shells. Never mind. With Hardy you always got the unexpected and this fit Hardy Bovine for sure. Not much of a fan of him and his ways. I reckon that's all I got to say about this confounded situation." He pulled the trigger and let Hardy fly.

Next up was prison guard Willy Sprigs. Steele eyed him curiously. He was a small framed scrawny little old man. He sported a waxed handlebar mustache that looked too large for his face. Sprigs wore a worn Stetson hat making him resemble a Wild West cowpoke throwback. All he needed was a pair of six shooters on his hips. Steele would have never figured him for a guard if he had seen him on the street. Willy eased off the hat and gripped it in both hands, bowed his head in silence before placing the hat back on his head.

"Hardy Bovine, what a hoot sending you off like this. I didn't have much use for you when you showed up at the prison. You were too much of a braggart and the boisterous type that rubbed me and a lot of others wrong with your 'my way' or the highway arrogant attitude. We had our rules and were doing just fine before you 'John Wayned' your butt in like you thought you owned the place. You left a bad taste in my mouth, one that no amount of brushing or gargling would flush. Who voted you sheriff? I stand here still surprised that you weren't 'kilt' dead by a guard the first week you were there. You rubbed salt in our wounds the way you treated the prisoners on your block like they had rights and all. They lost what society owed them when they committed the crimes that landed them there. I got plenty more I could say about it and about you, but I won't. This is your day, not mine to piss and moan." Willy Sprigs then pointed the gun almost straight in the air and fired. "Scattered, my part is done, amen and good riddance."

Steele took the shotgun from his hands. Willy eyed him, that look Steele had seen plenty of times; one that said, 'I don't give a damn about him or the horse he rode in on.' Steele scratched his head wondering why in the world Hardy had selected this bunch to be part of his send off. None of them liked him. Maybe he just figured they were good marksman. No need to try to figure out Hardy now; he was a hard read even when alive. Steele perused the four assembled in the field, five counting him. It didn't seem very respectful of a man that had died. There were no tears, no sad faces except from his real two friends. Why Hardy had chosen this way to go was anyone's guess. He certainly had left no explanation, just instructions. Steele peaked inside the box. There were three more shells to be fired yet. He would fire one, maybe Susan a second but which one of these scoundrels would he honor with a second round?

"Is this thing over with or not," spoke up Willy.

"Yeah, we don't have all day for this snipe shoot," added Skipper.

Hubert spoke his mind as well, "Hardy has had his day in the limelight. Consider him properly buried according to his last wishes. You're welcome by the way. I have chores that need tending. Rest in piece Hardy Bovine and if you can't you got nobody to blame but yourself."

Steele got his answer. None of these scoundrels were interested in firing a second round. He thought about shushing them until he paid his last respects but didn't see it worth the effort given how they felt about Hardy. He thanked them as they headed to their vehicles. Not so much as a grunt of a reply, they were done.

Susan stood there perplexed too, "That went well. Don't know them, never seem them before and if ever I see them again it will be too soon to suit me."

"I am just as confused as you why Hardy selected them to participate in this send off. Surely he had real friends somewhere."

"Steele, I think you are looking at his true friends. We're it minus Eddy. Why haven't you fired a Hardy shot by the way?"

"I intend to. I just figured there was no need keeping those fools around any longer."

"Fire when ready, I will be your witness."

Steele chambered a shell and then spoke his last words to commemorate his relationship with Hardy Bovine, "You were a hard man but a fair man. You were ornery but compassionate. You could be reserved yet vocal. The way you snookered us into this was deceitful but well orchestrated, well played indeed. People either liked or hated you, so it seems. We landed on the liking side of the fence. You were a straight shooter, even if you got there on your own time frame way too many times. You had unique perspectives and spoke them as you meant them. I can hear some of them clearly as you rattled them off: 'If you ride it, you feed it. If it drinks water it. If you open it, close it. If you borrow it return it. If you turn it on, turn it off. If you leave a mess, clean it up. If you fall, off get back on.' You lived by this cluster of what you called cowboy mantras. Seemed odd since you were not a cowboy and never owned a horse. You did your best to pass them on to us. I can still hear you professing things like: 'The past cannot be changed. Everybody's journey is different and there is no right or wrong way to get where you are going. Overthinking will never solve your problem. Kindness doesn't cost a plug nickel. True happiness is found on the inside first. You can only fail if you quit first. What goes around comes around and what you get is what you deserve.'

Susan interrupted him, "How do you remember all this stuff?"

"I spent more time with him than anyone else did. This is the closest I can get to anything scripture related. I read it someplace so here goes. Three men, three crosses, one hill. One man cursed, one man prayed, one man promised. One died condemned, one died forgiven, one died innocent. One died in sin, one died to sin, one died for sin. One was held by death, one was released by death, one conquered death. One lost life, one gained life, one was life. Thank you, Jesus, for your sacrifice and Praise God we have internal life, including the life of Hardy Bovine whose ashes have been scattered on this field." Steele took steady aim at nothing in particular and fired the gun. "Amen."

"Amen," repeated Susan as she cupped her arm underneath his. "I need to go home and see about Buttermilk. That cat hasn't been the same since Clabber ran used the last of her nine lives."

"Hardy always worried about those darn coyotes and I guess he was proven right. Clabber found a way to escape that corral and paid dearly for her Houdini high jinx."

"What about you, have you decided what you are going to do with Hardy's place and this land?"

"Well, it doesn't seem fitting to sell this acreage being it is his last resting place. It's kind of a cemetery now if you think about it. As for his home place, I am not sure. It's his house and all, not mine."

"A home is what you make of it, Steele. It is a prime spot right on the river and it is filled with wonderful memories."

"Don't you be trying to guilt me into keeping it gal. I have a place."

"But does it really feel like home?"

"It's a house. I sleep, cook and eat there. What else does a home have to be? Don't look at me like that, Susan. It was Hardy's notion and his notion only that I might marry and settle on his property and raise a family. I am perfectly happy living the life of a bachelor. I am taking a page out of the Hardy Bovine book. I don't need a woman ruining my life and telling me what I am supposed to do and what I can't. And before you try to convince me otherwise, step back and look at your life. You are an independent woman doing what you want to do when you want to do it. You are invested in that motorcycle shop just like I am in the machine shop. Why mess that up? Live, love it and leave marriage to those that need it to fill some black hole in their life."

Susan clapped her hands, "Well said. I will never bring up the subject again, too much the pot calling the kettle black."

"Let's get out of here. I'm over this funeral and shooting without targets involved."

"Rest peacefully Hardy Bovine," added Susan.

Every Beginning Deserves a Proper Ending

Two years had passed since that unique Hardy Bovine send off. Steele had locked up, the last employees having just exited McClain's Fabrication and Machine Shop. Red McClain pretty much allowed him to run the daily operations. Steele had even learned how to quote jobs and maintain the payroll. Red trusted him to do almost anything. Steele had adjusted to life without Hardy around but still missed his old friend. Not one needing much, he still owned his old pickup. No one had dared to ever mess with again. He did his best thinking during the long drive home. Today was no different.

Today he also thought about Eddy. The boy had died way too early, but he had lived life to the fullest. Even though he never inherited the fishing gear and the pontoon due to his untimely death before Hardy passed, he often visited, and he and Hardy would fish or just chew the fat. Hardy would never admit it, but Eddy was like a son, maybe more like a grandson to him. Steele chuckled, thinking about how Eddy had licked that chess grandmaster after just learning how to play. The chess grandmaster served to be a better teacher than player. He had taken it for granted that the checker playing boy on that porch could not beat him at his own game. No doubt, the guy never shared that experience with any of his cronies. Eddy would go down as the chess grandmaster of Pop's Country One Stop. One and done though, Eddy never took up the game. What did he really have to prove?

Steele was so lost in thought he almost missed his turn. He motored to the end of the drive and opted to sit a spell in the yard before going inside. It was a pleasant spring day and wasn't late enough for the state birds to be out and about. Mosquitoes were blood sucking vultures in these parts. Hardy called them skitters. Oddly, they never seemed to bite him. He credited it to him having leather tough skin and piss and vinegar running through his veins. Hardy had an answer for everything. You had to take them with a grain of salt though. He said an honest lie never hurt anybody. Steele would argue that there was no such thing as an honest lie. Hardy would just wink and say, 'prove it.' Hardy would often say, "if you are in fellowship, especially with the Lord, there is no need to worry about anything.' That always sounded peculiar coming from a man who never attended church or vowed to be a Christian. He wasn't shy about throwing God's name around when the situation called for it. Steele never heard him speak the Lord's name in vain.

Thinking about Hardy Bovine seemed to be occupying his downtime today. Hardy was good at reading a person's mood. If he seemed flustered, Hardy would remind him, 'Steele, stop focusing on how stressed you are and remember how blessed you are.' He indeed missed his old friend. His thoughts were interrupted by a familiar sound. He stood and watched as the origin of the noise came into view. He smiled seeing Susan dismount the Harley.

As she approached, she shrugged saying, "Sorry, had a new rebuild and we ran into a few hitches."

"Likely excuse," Steele replied as he pulled her into his arms and planted a wet one on her lips.

"Where's Buttermilk?"

"Oh, I haven't been inside. I just plopped in the swing enjoying what's left of the afternoon."

"It is beautiful out here. I'm glad you decided to keep it."

"I had no choice. Hardy cursed me saying it was the perfect place to marry and settle down and raise a family."

"I guess I can be thankful that you chose me for the wife part of that little curse."

"Friends and fellowship have a way of working out I reckon. I didn't see it coming until it arrived on a two-wheeler slap dab in my lap."

"I wish I could plead the fifth, but I was always attracted to you Lover. I valued our friendship though and didn't want to upset the apple cart. After Eddy and then Hardy died, it left just you and me. I figured the best way to seal our bond was to let my feelings be known. And here we are."

"You did catch me off guard with your revelation, but I quickly warmed up to it. I've been thinking."

"Should I run for the hills and hide, Steele Dillon?"

"You can but I have always been an excellent seeker. I especially have a bloodhound's nose when it comes to finding you. Just hear me out."

"All ears lay it on me."

****

It was their first wedding anniversary. They stood before God and repeated their vows. Steele kissed his bride and then handed her the shotgun. She fired the round into the field. Steeled reloaded and fired the second round. It seemed the perfect thing to do to seal the deal, their first year of marital bliss, firing those last two Hardy Bovine shells.

"Guns and ashes," whispered Steele.

"Guns and ashes," repeated Susan. "One for Hardy and one for Eddy, both for us."

An Author Nugget

Let's digress to the 60s. then high school student Tommy Winn, was in Mrs. Simmons English class. She tasked the class with writing a fictional short story, the subject of the story their choice. Little 'T' enjoyed playing chess. It was during the time of Bobby Fischer, a chess grandmaster, facing off against Boris Spassky of the USSR. Playing chess with cousins and friends was the perfect pastime for 'T' and ended up as the plot for his short story.

He penned his about a bus breaking down and becoming stranded at an old country store. A young lad sat on the front porch in front of checkerboard hopeful someone would come along and offer him a checker game. A chess grandmaster taught him how to play while waiting for the bus to be repaired. Sound familiar? Tommy completed his assignment, proud of the tale he had spun.

Judgement day arrived. Mrs. Simmons handed out the stories now graded. Tommy was shocked when his was marked with a large red 'F'. Devastated by this, an explanation was marked on the pages of the story. She had flunked him not because of the content or originally of his story but instead for his terrible spelling and punctuation. You see, 'T' had tried to portray the boy in the story as a county bumpkin using what he perceived to be slang southern language intentionally misspelled. Obviously, he didn't use proper punctuation either when expressing the dialogue. Dialogue was not required and he was probably the only one that used it. His teacher totally missed his intent. Apparently, Tommy had been ahead of his time, envisioning more depth than was required for a simple short story. Crushed, it would be a long time before he would wish to write again.

Redemption, 50 some odd years later, Eddy became that character who had originated in a simple short story. Take that, Mrs. Simmons.

About T. Allen Winn

Winn began writing in 2003 while being cooped up in hotels during business travel. Completing a 650 page so called novel he became hooked. The homegrown Abbeville, S.C. boy embraced the experience completing one novel and then leaping into the next one, fun and therapy at the time. That changed in 2011 when a chance encounter brought stranger and new neighbor Bob O'Brien to his Pawley's Island doorsteps. Bob did not realize the neighborhood home had been sold and apologized when Tom greeted him instead of the man he had expected to see. Book in hand, Bob had just published his first novel, The Toppled Pawn and explained the previous neighbor had shown interest in writing. Tom remarked he dabbled in writing to which Bob asked, do you have a manuscript? Tom replied 'ten'. Bob had just started Prose Press, a publishing company and suggested publishing one. You cannot make this stuff up.

T. Allen Winn's first novel, Road Rage joined the ranks of the published a few months later, and he owes a special thanks to Bob O'Brien for making this possible. His first seven books were published by Prose Press. In 2016, T. Allen Winn established Buttermilk Books, his publishing company. He has published thirty-three books. He and his wife reside in Myrtle Beach, South Carolina.

Ole T does not write a specific genre. He writes what strikes his fancy. If you don't see something that fits your reading wheelhouse, just tell him what you like, and he might just write it for you.

Books are available on Amazon or online where books are sold. Select books are available at Southern Succotash on Washington Street in Abbeville, S.C. and in Tabor City, N.C. at Grapefull Sisters Vineyard. Or *Message* T. Allen Winn on Facebook to arrange delivery of signed copies, or to schedule him to speak at an event or book club.

Fiction from T. Allen Winn

The Perfect Spook House

Dark Thirty

Lou Who

Raw Ride, a Wild West Zombie Apocalyptic Shoot'um Up

The Man Who Met the Mouse

Mister Twix Mystery, a Cat Scene Investigation

Come Here, Getouttahere, Tyler's Tail Wagging Tale

The Tenth Elemental

Last Stand on the Grand Strand

The Lord's Last Acres

Covert 19, 2020 A Devil of a Year

The Sot and The Savior

Outside the Clique

The Detective Trudy Wagner series

Road Rage
North of the Border
Tithes and Offerings
Trudy Wagner, Southern Belle, the Prequel to Road Rage

Bigfoot Trilogy

Book 1: Foot, Tree Knockers and Rock Throwers

Book 2: Another Foot, What Really Happened to
D.B. Cooper
Book 3: Final Foot, Willow Creek

Non-Fiction from T. Allen Winn

Being Bentley, A Dog Like No Other

December's Darkest Day, While I Breathe, I Hope

The Hardwood Walker of
Port Harrelson Road (based on true events in
Bucksport, S.C.)

Cuz, My Brother, Life is Good, God is Good

Memoirs

The Caregiver's Son, Outside the Window Looking In

Vol 1: Cornbread and Buttermilk, Good Ole Fashion Home
Cooked Nostalgic Nonsense

Vol 2: Don't Sit Naked in a Grits Tree, More
Nostalgic Nonsense

Pushed Into The Pull, Thank You Cuz

The Endless Mulligan, Short Shots from the Golf Whomper

Abbeville Football with Co-Author Benji Greeson

It's All About the 'A', Faith, Family, Football and
Forever to Thee
It's All About the Angels in the Backfield, Dawn of a
Dynasty

Biographies

Clay Page, Somewhere In Between

Screw It, Let's Ride, The Legend Bub Lollis

Short Stories

For Your Amusement featured in Beach Author Network's book titled 'Shorts'

Ciled Me a Bar featured in friend and author, Danny Kuhn's Headline Book's *Mountain Mysts*, Honorable Mention in Fiction at the 2015 London Book Festival and the book is endorsed by *Joyce Dewitt* of the sitcom *Three's Company*

Short story about Granny Bowie in friend and author Robert Sharpe's book, *The Heart and Soul of Caring*, about caregivers and their challenges

www.ingramcontent.com/pod-product-compliance
Lightning Source LLC
Chambersburg PA
CBHW060219180626
46813CB00007B/2889